VAMPIRE GIRL 7: FALLEN STAR

KARPOV KINRADE

DARING BOOKS

To my brother, Neil. May you find your peace. I miss you. ~Lux, forever your big sister

And to the friends who have become family and the family who are friends. You make our lives complete.
~Lux & Dmytry KK

ALEX STONE

*Y*ou may be wondering what a girl like me is doing in a place like this. Dark. Damp. Filled with mummified corpses too old to name. Creepy crawlies that you don't even want to know about. *Crunch* Ew. I think I just crushed one with my palm.

Give me a sec while I wipe the goo off my hands.

Even the dust smells like it's lived and died a thousand times since the last human stepped foot in here.

And yet here I am, cobwebs in my hair, bug goo oozing into the cracks of my fingers despite my best effort to rub the crap off on the stone, crawling on my hands and knees through a narrow tunnel that should lead me to a cavern.

'Should' being the operative word here.

Well, let me set the record straight. First, I'm not a girl, I'm a woman. Notice the date on my driver's license? Fully fledged grown-up. Also, those two PhDs at the end of my name are hard to come by as a girl. Factor in that I got my degrees by the age of twenty-five, and you can perhaps understand why I don't like being called girl. I graduated high school at sixteen. College at eighteen. Two PhDs in six years seemed a bit behind the curve, to be honest. I'm still bummed about that.

But life is full of little disappointments, isn't it?

The question is, will this tomb be a disappointment as well, or will we finally find what we've been scouring the world for?

"See anything, Alex?" Trevor's voice startles a critter near my foot, who makes a dash for my legs and tries to shimmy up my pants. Jokes on him, though. I learned long ago to keep that shit tucked in tight. That was a life lesson best not repeated. I still have the scars as a reminder.

Not finding a way in, the little beast screeches and scurries away. Probably to tell his friends all about the two delicious morsels waiting in the wings.

Trevor and I being those morsels, in case that was unclear.

"Nothing yet," I answer, trying to keep my voice low so as not to disturb whatever else might be living here.

While my partner might not believe anything that science can't definitively prove, I've seen enough to know we don't know everything. In fact, we don't know much at all. And not to toot my own horn, but I know a whole hell of a lot, so that's saying something.

Trevor's never been on an excavation like this before. He has no clue that's the real reason his company hired me. He thinks I'm here to fulfill some kind of PC vagina quota. That we're just searching for a rare artifact worth a lot of money. Something that museum's worldwide will drool over. Something that will unlock a few more secrets of the past.

Nothing wrong with that (err…, except for the vagina quota bullshit. I refer you back to my double PhDs). For the rest, well, we've all got to start somewhere.

But, I know better.

I know what we seek holds power. Real power.

Power I can't let Global Tech get their hands on. Which is the only reason I took this gig. To double-cross them.

I know, not very sportsmanlike. But if you knew what was at stake, you'd do the same. Trust me.

Plus, they're not the only ones after it. Dr. Vane's team— an archaeologist of questionable repute who has beaten me to more than a few precious finds—is en route as we speak, according to sources who know shit. I can't let that old man get his hands on this. Way too dangerous for someone with ties to not-quite-legal organizations who are known to smuggle rare artifacts into other countries and sell them to private collectors on the black market. If I ever meet the greedy son of a bitch in person, I have a few choice words to share with him. But, alas, he keeps a low profile.

I do too, but not for nefarious reasons. I do it mostly for my reputation. As young as I am, I look even younger. I'm working at reaching 5'5", but can only manage with heels, I'm compact—or what some would call 'scrappy' and my short pale blonde hair usually features a few fun colors. I get carded a lot. My look doesn't help instill respect and clout in a middle-aged white dude's club. So, I stay off social media, keep my pictures out of newspapers and online write-ups, and let my work speak for itself. Most people mistake me for a middle-aged white dude. Imagine their surprise!

I squint as the darkness that edges around the thin beam of light from my headlamp begins to brighten, and I feel a shift in the air around me. "We're coming up to something," I say.

Trevor grunts in response, and a few more critters frolic around our hands. Something bites the thick part of my palm, and I hold back a curse and smash the bastard against the stone, feeling it's small bones break. I can't move my head enough to look at my hand, but I feel blood pooling. I'll have

3

to get something on that soon. Who knows what kind of infections these creatures carry.

I slow my pace, knowing I could be crawling into a trap. And then I stop completely and suddenly, my heart a drum against my ribs. Trevor bumps into me.

"What's the holdup?"

I look down, and my light doesn't carry far. If I'd kept going, I would have crawled off the edge into total darkness. "We've got a bit of a problem," I tell him. "But I have a plan."

It's not a great plan. But it's a plan. I explain it, and though I can't see his face, I know the look he's giving me.

He didn't like giving up control of this excavation to a 'girl.' He was also expecting a dude. But we worked it out. And in the course of things somehow ended up in bed.

Probably a mistake. But a fun one, I will admit. I'd like to say it had nothing to do with his sculpted body, dark bedroom eyes and wicked grin, but I'd be lying. I'm still a woman, after all. I have needs.

And in a job like mine, I take the fun where it can be had.

Still, our roll in the hay didn't erase the sharp edges of misogyny embedded in Trevor's DNA. So this plan isn't an easy sell.

Fortunately, I don't need his permission. He can join, or stay on his hands and knees and wait for me to discover the artifact and claim the credit. You want to bet he'll stay and wait?

Didn't think so.

I pull out two climbing picks and prepare for the crazy part. This is where it gets tricky, because I have very little room to maneuver, I don't know what's below us, and all manner of shit could hit the proverbial fan.

In one fluid movement, I slam the picks into the rock, launch myself out of the shaft I'd been crawling through, and spin around so I'm now facing a wall of stone as I hang from the picks for dear life.

"I'm going down," I tell Trevor, who's now watching me from the position I was just in. His eyes are wide, pupils slightly dilated, though that could be the headlamp shining directly into them. He's definitely never been on a dig like this. He fancied himself Indiana Jones. It didn't occur to him I would be the hero in this story.

Okay, so this next part isn't very exciting. Show don't tell. I know, I know. But seriously, do you really want to hear about how I pull out one pick, move it down an inch or two, ram it back into the stone, and keep doing that over and over as my muscles burn and sweat drips down my face and pools under my arms, and in just about every other crack of my body? Yeah, it's not glamorous. If they make a movie, it'll be a lot more exciting, I'm sure. Until then, let's skip to the good part.

By the way, I totes want the young Lara Croft actress to play me, okay? She's a total badass. Now that we've got that handled…

My foot finally lands on something solid. This is where shit gets real. "You're almost there," I tell Trevor, who looks like he needs some encouragement. He only has one PhD, so you know how it goes.

I'm just kidding about that. Most PhDs I know can't do this. Wouldn't want to do this. No matter how many they've collected. This is crazy. I'm crazy. But you probably figured that out already.

And Trevor isn't so bad. He's a product of his own privilege for sure, but then who isn't?

The key is some degree of self-awareness. Being woke, as they say. Trevor is anything but woke.

With both feet finally on solid ground, I exhale gratefully, letting my legs take more of my body's weight as I ease up on my arms. But I don't let go of my picks.

Not yet, anyway.

Why, you ask?

Clearly you've never been in a situation where the ground fell out from under your feet and the only things that saved your life were the climbing picks you held onto. But I don't hold that against you.

Even my closest friends think I'm total craycray.

So I hold on as I let more weight drop onto the floor beneath me. Another critter crunches under my boot. I feel no pity or remorse for its demise.

I pull one pick out of the stone while keeping hold of the other one with my right hand. "So far so good," I tell Trevor, who hasn't dared venture this close to the ground yet. "I'm going to let go and see if it holds."

"You sure about that?" he asks.

"Sure as I'll ever be."

And so I pull my other pick out but stay close to the stone wall, ready to slam my picks back into the rock the moment I feel the earth beneath me shift.

It doesn't. Hooray for me.

Carefully, I turn around to face the cavern.

I never know what to expect. Every discovery is different. Will this have monsters? Treasure? Dust bunnies? A little bit of each? It's anyone's guess.

This one is… empty.

Empty?

I squint, searching more carefully.

Yup. Empty.

Well, shit.

"Um, Trevor, we might have another problem."

He lowers himself next to me, still facing the wall. His

body is so close our shoulders brush against each other, and I wait to see if I feel that zing of attraction I felt before.

Nope. Fizzled already. Ah, well. These things never do last long.

"What problem?" he asks, breathless.

"See for yourself."

He turns slowly and then curses. "There's nothing here."

"That was my first thought too. But... we might be wrong." An idea is forming in my head. And so I slide my picks into their custom-made slots in my pants (what, yours don't have those?) and creep forward, into the center of the circular room. The wall reaches higher than I can see, with a great black emptiness above us. There are small crevices that break up the wall, like the one we snuck through, but otherwise it's giant and unending. The floor is a series of square stones in different shades of ochre and gray.

I find the center of the room and stand there, staring at my feet.

Trevor stays by the wall, presumably to be helpful, I'm sure. "See anything?" he asks, a nervous tremor in his voice.

Again, not judging, just reporting it like it is.

But I don't respond, because in fact, I do see something. The outline around the center stone is deeper and the grooves are more prominent compared to the rest of the floor. And that makes me wonder.

So I pace around it, my brain whirling, as pieces fall into place. Colors. Puzzles. Lines. Differences. Everything I observe clicking into a new order as I move the information around in my mind.

Until it snaps together and I laugh out loud. "Of course! Like in Budapest only with color."

"Budapest? What the hell are you going on about, Alex?"

I wave a hand at him dismissively and get to work, stepping on different stones in different configurations as I suss out the puzzle.

It takes time, but I am patient (oh, shut it. I am. When it counts.) Trevor paces impatiently (see, that's what it looks like to not be patient. Very different from *moi*, no?) Finally, I solve the riddle and jump back as the center stone begins to push itself up from the floor.

Under the stone is a compartment that holds the glowing fragment of what was once a perfect orb. But this is only a piece of the original orb. Global Tech thought they were getting the whole thing. Bam! Instant power. But I knew we would only find a piece.

How, you ask, could I possibly know that?

Because… I have one of the pieces. Shh… that's a secret no one but you and I know. I first discovered it after my parents were murdered when I was twelve. It was in a hidden vault under our Malibu mansion.

Which leaves a few more pieces out there. This is my life's work. This is what my parents died protecting and what I will risk my life to find.

I pull a canvas bag of rice out of my pocket. It happens to weigh exactly what this orb piece weighs. What an unlikely coincidence. Taking no chances—because of course I've seen Indiana Jones—I transfer the rice bag to the pedestal as I remove the orb, holding my breath and moving with cat-like grace.

When the transfer is complete, I look down in awe at the pulsing moon-like crevice slightly larger than my hand as the power it holds begins to pour through me. Closing my eyes, I open myself to its history.

Here's where I tell you my real secret. Promise you won't tell? Especially Mr. Wanna-Be-Jones here? Okay. Here it is.

I don't think I'm entirely human.

I mean, don't get me wrong. I look as human as they come. All the parts in all the appropriate places.

And I have the full range of human emotions.

But… I also can do things other humans can't.

Like read objects. I can touch an object and see its history. Where it's been. What it can do. What it's done.

It's my cheat. The reason I'm the best at what I do.

So, now you know. Hopefully we can still be friends. Cuz I dig you.

Get it? *Dig* you. Little archeology joke there.

So back to the orb. It's singing to me. Telling me its secrets. Showing me where I can find the last piece. But before I get the whole story, its voice is silenced.

As Trevor yanks it out of my hand.

I open my eyes and glare at him. "What the hell?"

He's now staring at it wide-eyed. "What makes it glow?"

"You know how rude that was?" I reach to take it back, but he pulls it away from me.

"Just give me a sec," he whines—and there is nothing more attractive than a grown man whining, am I right, ladies? "Besides, shouldn't you figure out a way out?"

Well, he's got a point there. If I rely on him, we'll die together in here, and I'm not spending the rest of my life— and all of my afterlife—with a one-night stand.

I glare at him a moment more, my instincts screaming at me to take the orb back and tuck it away safely where it belongs. But he's been working hard to find this thing, and I'm going to be ruining his career when I steal it from both him and Global Tech, so… whatever. I'll let him have his moment of glory.

As he said, I need to find a way out. Preferably one that doesn't require us scaling the wall we climbed down and crawling through the hall of bugs again.

I'm guessing there's another trick that will open a door.

So I study the tiles and put my thinking cap on. Meanwhile, Trevor's eyes are glued to the orb piece.

I have a lightbulb moment and wonder if it's too simple to work. But worth a try, am I right? I reverse my walk on the tiles that opened the secret compartment, and the middle tile returns into the ground. As it does, a piece of stone wall grinds against itself, peeling open a door that hadn't been there before.

Voila. We have an exit. I hold out my hand for the orb, and Trevor gives it back to me reluctantly then follows me to the door.

"Careful where you step," I say. "There are likely many booby traps still lurking around here."

"I'm not an idiot, Alex. I know what I'm doing."

Someone's getting testy. But I hold my tongue. See how diplomatic I can be? But of course, as he steps out of the chamber, pushing in front of me to do so, he nearly triggers said booby trap. One of the tiles is a different shade than the rest. I grab him and pull him back, then point. "That could have killed us," I tell him harshly, all patience wearing thin.

"You don't even know that's a trap," he says with more whine. Want any cheese with that, dude?

"Do you want to risk it when we're this close to getting out of here?"

He frowns at me. "Are we really that close?"

I nod and point down the corridor we just entered, showing him how this is where we started. "Just down that hall is the ladder we climbed down from the surface."

He smiles, and there's a glint in his eyes I don't like.

I don't see the knife in his hand until it's too late.

Until it's pushed into my gut. "Sorry about this, Alex. But I can't let you get all the credit, or turn this over to Global Tech. There are buyers willing to pay big for whatever this glowing bit is, and I intend to retire in wealth."

He pulls the artifact out of my pocket and pushes me backwards, onto the discolored tile I just warned him about.

Then he runs, coward that he is. He runs down the path I had to point out to him, while I fall, a knife sticking out of my gut. He makes it out just as my heel pushes on the tile unleashing the trap I knew was there.

Rushing water fills the cavern.

Oh joy. I love the suspense of how will Alex die today? Blood loss, internal injuries, or drowning?

ALEX STONE

*I*t's not as fun as you might think, being right all the time.

At the moment I'm literally drowning in how right I was.

Also, that asshole was so not worth sleeping with. I really need to reevaluate my taste in men. Celibacy is looking like a much more valid life choice.

I've left the knife in my gut for now, because taking it out could be more deadly. At least for the moment the knife is stemming the blood loss a bit. Every drop I can keep on the inside of my body is a small win for me.

The water is rising quickly, and I will soon run out of room for my head. I have maybe three minutes until I'm completely submerged with no way to breathe. Because, of course, setting off this trap also closed the exit just as Trevor-the-weasel slipped out with my treasure.

I'll deal with him later. First, I have to get out of here alive.

Think, Alex. Think.

I look around, assessing the space. The water is coming from below. Maybe there's a way out under me? I kick my feet, and the use of core muscles sends shooting pain through my body, but I do my best to ignore it. It's not worse than that time a corpse came alive and bit me. Good thing it wasn't contagious. But damn that took time to heal. And it's not exactly something one can easily explain at the hospital. I had to rely on a good friend of mine to fix me up. A situation that has become commonplace over the years of adventures. My friend is… well, I don't exactly know what she is. But she never bats an eye at my stories, and always have the perfect remedy for the strange injuries and ailments I bring back from my job. There's definitely something paranormal going on with her, but she's a pretty private person and I don't like to pry.

At any rate, she's the reason I'm still alive.

For now, at least.

Despite strong swimming skills (fun fact: I could have been an Olympic contender, but I had bigger fish to fry) I make very little progress trying to reach the bottom. The influx of water is too strong and pushes me away. Instead, I go with the flow and see where that takes me.

Experience dictates there should be some way of reversing this or escaping. Some kind of puzzle to solve. Or monster to fight.

I'm hoping for a puzzle.

The water slams me against a stone wall, and I grip it and let my power flow through me and into the stone.

"Come on, tell me something, anything that will get me out of here."

I have no actual evidence that talking to things makes my power work better, but it makes me feel better, so there's that.

A feeling like lightning surges through my skin and I follow the impulse to where it's stronger, tracing my hands across the wall as I tread water. Ignoring the pain building in my torso, I keep my head above water, so to speak. And then I find it.

The puzzle.

The riddle, actually.

It's already submerged under water, the words etched into the stone in an ancient language that no one in my profession would recognize as human.

Luckily I'm a bit of a self-taught genius when it comes to the paranormal elements of archaeology.

That and my power helps.

I push myself under water, sucking in enough air to fill my lungs as I do, and face the wall. I let my fingers run over the hieroglyphs, feeling the meaning even as my brain translates from my time studying this.

Blood from my blood.

Bone from my bone.

Feed me your life.

Live in your death.

It loses some of its poetry in translation, but you get the idea. I memorize the riddle and kick up to get in some much-needed air as my lungs nearly collapse. The electricity of power is still surging through me, and my head is swimming from lack of oxygen, blood loss, and adrenaline.

It's the adrenaline that's likely keeping me alive at this point.

I suck in air and puzzle out the words I just read.

It doesn't take me long to piece together that this wall wants my blood. Which is great. I might actually have a little left on the inside of my body.

No problemo.

Question is, how do I give it my blood? The water is already red with my dwindling life force. That's not making any magic shit happen. So now what?

I dive back under and feel about the wall for something… anything that could potentially suck out my blood.

See how fun my job is?

Aren't you super jelly?

There's one spot different from the rest. It's a circular groove that looks as if it could move, with the right motivation.

I'm running out of air, so I let my power flow, and it directs me to the right, where another smaller stone is wedged into the wall. Like a button.

Couldn't be that easy, could it?

I press the stone button, and the first groove caves inward, revealing a dark hole.

Blood and bone.

Blood and bone.

Oh shit.

Okay, kids, close your eyes. What comes next isn't pretty.

Because I have a feeling I know how it's going to get my blood, and it's going to hurt like a mother fu—

Well, you get the idea.

I stick my arm into the dark hole.

And then something inside drills down into my flesh and bone.

Nope, not exaggerating. The wall is literally getting the blood from my gods be damned bone.

I bite back a scream, because I'm underwater and don't want to drown.

But there's only so much pain even I can handle.

As something sucks out my blood and bone and bone marrow, I feel the walls around me shift. The water begins to move in a new direction.

But I don't stay conscious long enough to notice.

* * *

15

My consciousness is fleeting, but somewhere deep down I have a sense of time passing. Of heat blazing against my pale skin, burning it. Of clothes turning from wet and cold to dry and brittle. Of sand against my flesh and bugs exploring what they must think is a new carcass.

They might be right.

I can't hold onto my thoughts for long, or my consciousness, but I know enough to realize I'm dying. Well and truly dying.

The dagger to the gut didn't kill me.

Drowning didn't kill me.

But now…

I'm done for.

I'd like to tell you my life flashes before my eyes.

That I see all the magical moments I've lived. A light at the end of the tunnel. God.

Nothing like that.

I do, however, see the one thing I want more than anything in the world.

I see my parents.

Looking just as they did the night they were murdered.

They were so happy that night. Celebrating a lead role my dad landed for a new movie. They dressed up, and I got to wear my fancy new gown, and we went out to our favorite restaurant. We laughed and talked and they listened to everything I had to say about my day, down to the fight my best friend and I had gotten into. (She was playing with another girl in class and I was sad and jealous.)

They gave me advice and helped me feel better.

I thought my life could never be happier.

And I was right. I've never been happier than I was that night.

When we got home, it wasn't immediately clear something was wrong. I could sense something bad was about to happen. I told them. Told them the door to our mansion had warned me. (I didn't have full control or understanding of my powers yet, so I sometimes sounded a bit mental.)

They thought I was tired. That my imagination was getting away from me. They tucked me in and kissed me goodnight. Smiling.

When I woke to the screaming, I knew that was it. They were dying, and I only saw a brief glimpse of the monster who killed them.

Their blood dripped from his lips, staining his teeth.

They lay in a heap next to each other, pale corpses that resembled the people I loved more than anything.

He'd drained them.

The cops were perplexed, but put no stock in a barely twelve-year-old's theories of vampires lurking in the streets of Malibu. It was ludicrous.

But now, as my life slips away, I see them again, as they were when they tucked me in. My mom's blue eyes, lit up with joy, her dark hair falling in waves around her pale face. My dad with his movie star looks, blond and tan, telling me a story, his green eyes crinkling when he laughs.

I'll be with them again. That's not a bad thing, I think. Dying isn't such a bad thing after all.

The pain in my body is fading. The heat from the day has dissipated, and I am bathed in the cool embrace of the moon as I fade away.

I feel my parent's hands grip each of mine. *I'm ready,* I tell them.

But they fade before my eyes, their faces sad, their arms reaching for me, but not reaching me.

And then they are gone.

A scream tears out of my throat, raw and visceral it claws through my body and into the wide void of life before me.

"Is this normal?" a woman's voice asks.

"There is no normal," a male British voice replies. "But it appears to have worked, so that's good news."

My eyes open, letting in light that feels painfully bright but is actually the dim flames of a fire. I try to sit up, but my body feels as if it's been run through by a herd of angry bulls.

"Easy there. You've been through an ordeal." That same sexy British voice is talking to me again, but I can't see the face attached to it. All I see are stars. Stars dotting a night sky in constellations that are unfamiliar to me.

I feel the man come closer and my body tenses as his arm slides behind my shoulders to help me sit up.

He holds a cup to my mouth, and I realize I am more thirsty than I've ever been in my entire life. Not just thirsty, but like a hungry-thirst. Like I will die if I don't drink whatever is in this cup, because it smells delicious and I'm nearly hallucinating with the promise of its pleasure.

"Drink up. You'll feel infinitely better once you do. Then we'll talk."

I blink. My eyes filling with tears, though I don't know why. Then I drink.

The viscous liquid coats my throat and feels so good going down that I want to sing and dance and laugh, but mostly I want to keep drinking.

When the cup empties the last of its god-like wonder into my mouth I nearly cry like a child deprived of their favorite toy. What the blazes is wrong with me? I'm never this much of an emotional scatterbrain. Must be a side-effect of a near-death experience, though I've had my share of those and never felt like this.

The dreams I had are starting to come back to me. Of seeing my dead parents.

It stirs an ache in my heart that temporarily replaces my desire for more of that drink.

But then my thirst comes back, and the man holding me

up—who's face I still haven't seen—laughs in a very throaty, sexy way as he replaces my cup with a fresh, full cup.

I keep drinking. I don't even care that I don't know where I am or who I'm with or what the bloody hell happened.

I'm happy.

And when I reach the end of this cup, I am finally satiated.

It's then that I notice my pain is gone.

Like… completely.

That's… impossible.

And the dimness of the night suddenly seems as clear and crisp as day, though I know it's still the middle of the night.

What's happening to me?

I turn and prop myself up to face the man who's been feeding me the liquid of the gods. The man with the dreamy British accent. And I suck in my breath when I see his face.

He is easily the most unbelievably sexiest man I have ever seen in my life. And that includes every movie star you can imagine. Take the top three most swoon-worthy movie stars you can think of, blend them into something even more jaw-dropping, keep doubling that until you can't anymore, and you're still not getting the picture here.

This man—who's not wearing a shirt by the way—oozes sex and beauty and charm and charisma. Golden hair like a Greek god. Blue eyes that shine in his face like sapphires. A chiseled chin and a six-pack you could grate cheese on. His smile is the death of me, and the bastard knows it.

"Welcome back to the land of the living. I'm Dean. And you must be the esteemed Dr. Alex Stone."

I feel tongue-tied, but somehow manage to find words. "Yes, I'm Alex. Who are you again?"

He holds out his hand to shake mine, and despite the oddity of it all, my professional manners kick in and I shake his hand.

19

His smile glows even brighter, if you can imagine that. "Dr. Dean Vane at your service. I must say I was expecting someone older. And… more male."

My eyeballs practically pop out of my head. "*You're* Dr. Vane? The pompous, middle-aged pseudo-scientist who's been pillaging my finds and corrupting our field with unethical practices?"

I pull my hand out of his, despite how luscious his skin feels against mine, and he chuckles. The bastard chuckles. "I see my reputation proceeds me. I assure you my degrees are real. And only a fraction of what you've heard is true. But you… " he gives me a look like he knows every secret fantasy I've ever thought and is ready, right here and now, to fulfill them. "You are a delightful surprise. Rumor has it *you* are the middle-aged man creating quite a stir in archaeological communities. I wasn't expecting… this!" His eyes glow with a kind of desire I should be used to in men, but this is different. Very different. And it makes my body stand up and take attention, despite my professional loathing of him.

I struggle to remember my very recent vows of celibacy.

He chuckles again. "Though I didn't expect to find you quite so… well… dead."

All sexy thoughts vanish at his words, as panic wells in me. "Dead?"

"Why, yes. Well, very nearly at any rate. If you'd been fully dead it would have been out of my hands entirely. You had just enough life left that I could bring you back. Though it was a close call. We weren't sure you'd make it even then."

"I… uh… how exactly did you bring me back?"

And then I look at the cups I just guzzled like my life depended on it. And I lick my lips and really taste what it was I've been drinking.

Thick.

Viscous.

Iron and salt.

Red.

Blood.

I pull away from him with reflexes I never had before tonight. "What have you done to me?"

I ask, but I already know. Because I'd long suspected what the enigmatic Dean Vane really was.

Rumors spread.

He only travels at night.

His name appears in journals far older than any human has any right to be.

He targets paranormal artifacts, which is why it's so hard to believe we've never run into each other. But he keeps such a low profile.

Like he has a secret to hide.

He shrugs, as if this is no big deal. "I had no choice really. You would have died."

I look down at my hands, and they are more pale than normal. My skin more perfect than it ever has been. Everything in me feels different. More alive, ironically. More attuned to every scent, every change in the wind, every sound. I'm a predator. A hunter. A monster.

"Did you turn me into a vampire?"

ALEX STONE

"*N*o need to be maudlin about it, my dear. It wouldn't be the end of the world. But no, I didn't need to turn you. Though it was a close call. I did, however, have to feed you copious amounts of my blood to keep you alive. You're welcome, by the way." He smiles, but I am not charmed.

Well, I'm trying really, really hard not to be charmed. Damn him and his... magnetism. It's incredibly difficult to stay mad a man you want to... well, explore. If you catch my drift.

Can't get too detailed here, in case some young ones are reading this. But you grown-ups, you can fill in the blanks, I'm sure. Or just watch the opening credits of True Blood and you'll get the idea.

I definitely want to do bad things to this man.

This... no, not man. Vampire. Monster.

The thing that killed my parents.

That ruined my life.

That... saved my life?

"I drank vampire blood?" I ask, suddenly feeling like I'm going to vomit.

"And quite a lot of it. I've never seen anything like it, to be honest. Are you sure you're entirely human?" he raises an eyebrow at me, and my heart pounds against my ribs in alarm.

"Of course, why would you even ask such a thing?" He can't know my secret. The secret I don't even fully know. No one but me and my friend know the truth about what I am— and she has her own secrets.

He leans into me and inhales deeply, his face coming close to my neck. "My blood has changed your scent, but before, when you were bleeding out... let's just say the last human girl I met who smelled this delicious turned out to be more than human. You don't smell like her, but you smell... different."

I scoot away from him, though the feel of his body so close to mine sends shivers through my spine. Traitorous body. "Why do I feel so different? What did your blood to do me?"

He frowns. "It shouldn't have done anything to you, other than heal you. Vampire blood doesn't give powers or change people. It can heal mortal wounds. That's it. Why? What are you feeling?"

Again he looks suspicious, and I know I need to change the subject. I check my body to see how it's doing. There's a bloody shirt wrapped around my arm where the stone wall sunk its teeth into me. I pull it off carefully, expecting to see open wounds, but the skin is completely healed. Only fading scars remain.

"Those should mostly heal, with time," he says.

I just nod as I look down at my abdomen, where a knife was recently jutting out of me. Traitorous Trevor. But my stomach is smooth once more, save another fading scar.

"That's… " I don't have words. But I do have a question. "Why?" I ask, my eyes full of accusations. "Why did you save me? What do you want?"

Before you judge me too harshly for being ungrateful and for not falling into the arms of the sexy vampire, let me first say, I get it, okay? I get that there's a whole new fad of loving vampires. Of wanting to be them or be with them at least. I know there are gaggles of girls—and women—everywhere who would kill to be in my position right now.

But they didn't see their parent's lifeless bodies mere moments after a vampire drained them.

They didn't see the cold, dead look in that vampire's eyes as it walked away covered in their parent's blood.

They don't know what it's like to wake up with night-mares about having the blood sucked out of your body while you scream, but no one can hear you.

And now I have a vampire's blood flowing through me. Now, I am indebted to the kind of creature that ruined my life.

And it's changed me. I can feel it. Maybe it's not supposed to. But maybe because I'm something more than human it woke something up inside me, and I'm terrified by that. And angry. And suspicious. Wouldn't you be? Keep in mind my partner and former lover did just stab me in the gut and leave me for dead. Can you blame me for being on my guard?

Dr. Vane grins and stands, offering me a hand to join him.

I refuse his assistance, but I do stand. Slowly. Cautiously. I expect to feel weak, tired, in pain… but instead I am filled with energy and mental clarity. I smile at the sensation, taking a brief moment from the madness to offer a quiet thanks to whatever gods may be that I am still alive.

Glancing at the sexy archaeologist standing in front of me, my smile and gratitude fade. I'm alive, but at what cost?

"I'm still waiting for my answer," I remind him. "What do you want from me?"

"Come this way Dr. Stone, and I will show you."

My night vision is sharpened and my myopic focus expands to take in my surroundings for the first time since consciousness returned.

I expected to find myself in the desert. Somewhere outside of Azekah in Israel, to be exact. But what I see is... well, it's nearly indescribable.

I'm standing in the center of a mighty grove of trees, thick branches swaying in a warm breeze that smells of forest with a hint of floral notes. We seem to be situated around the largest tree, and without thought I reach out to lay my palm on its bark, closing my eyes. As I do, I can feel the roots of the tree digging deep into the soil, the tips of the branches reaching for the sky, extending towards the stars, and I hear its heartbeat. That's the best way I can describe it. The pulse that gives it life. That pumps life into the world around it. And like a very old woman opening her eyes slowly, the tree wakes and looks at me. No, not *at* me, *into* me. And I feel it communicating with me. Not with words, exactly, but with some kind of emotional language that far outdates the limitation of words. But I understand the message.

I open my eyes, tears filling them, spilling onto my cheeks, though I barely notice and care even less.

"She's scared," I say. "They're all scared. Why?"

Dr. Vane raises an eyebrow at me. "How do you know that?"

"She told me," I say, my mind still in a haze. I see the grove with fresh eyes now. I see the invisible connections between the roots and the plants and the animals that scurry about, as if the underlying pattern of the world has just become clear. Its transposed itself over reality, in lines and swirls of glowing blue.

I blink, and it disappears, but somehow I know I can bring it back again. That a new part of my gift has been awakened.

By him, I realize, staring at the vampire before me. "Where are we?" I ask, with less anger than I would have had a few moments ago.

"We are in my world," Dr. Vane says. "Inferna. I brought you here because I feared I could not save you in the desert. This grove has its own magic, an ancient magic that goes back to the time before our kind ruled here. I felt you needed to be here in order to survive. It wasn't just my blood you drank," he says, cocking his head. "It was mixed with the sap from this tree. The Mother Tree. She saved you."

My eyes water again as those feelings of connecting with her wash over me. "She has been through great pain," I say. "Many years ago."

He nods. "There was an accident. A misuse of power. This grove was nearly destroyed. But her roots run deep and through time and the power of the Earth Druid, we were able to bring her back to full power."

"But now she's in danger," I say. It's not a question, though I don't know why. She doesn't know why.

"Yes," he says. "And I think your employer is behind that danger." His voice tightens in disapproval.

I spin on him. "If you're talking about Global Tech, they aren't my employer."

"But they did pay you to find Nirandel's Star, did they not?"

"To find what?"

He sighs, clearly exasperated. "The artifact you were after. They sponsored the dig, yes?"

"Yes, but I was using them. I was never going to give it to them. Unfortunately, that was also my partner's plan. He betrayed me at the last moment, leaving me for dead."

"I figured something along those lines when you turned up with a knife in the gut," he says.

I wince at the memory of that moment. Of the pain, but also, the betrayal.

"What do you know about Global Tech? About their plans?"

"Come," he says. "Let's go inside. You might want a bath and some food. There is much to discuss. It's a pity you lost the piece you had. That's a dangerous weapon in the wrong hands."

My mind snaps back, pulling out of the haze the Mother Tree put me in, as his words sink in and take hold and the truth of what he's said hits me hard. "Wait. Hold up. You're talking about this place like it isn't part of earth. Like it's a different world entirely."

He grins, winking at me as if this was a bar and not... well, whatever it actually is. "Did you really believe earth was the only inhabitable world? There's a lot you don't know about the universe, Doctor. And Earth isn't the only game in town."

He's walking at a brisk pace, and I have no choice but to keep up or be left alone in the grove, not that I would mind. But my breath hitches when we move out of the trees and onto a cobbled, moss-covered path that leads to... "Is that a castle?"

He nods, clear pride glowing on his face. "Welcome to my realm," he says. "One of seven in Inferna." He gestures to the towering castle before us. "And that is the Pleasure Palace."

"The Pleasure Palace? Are you for real? That's the best you could do?" Corny name aside, it's extraordinary. Made of what looks like quartz crystal with hues of peach and pale pink, with rounded towers at each of the four corners It glistens under the bright gaze of the moon—correction, moons!

27

I look up and am astonished to see two moons hanging heavy in the clear sky.

"We really are on another world," I whisper, all doubt erased even as my mind boggles at it all.

"Is it really so hard to believe?" Dr. Vane asks. "You clearly know about the paranormal on your world, so you already have a more open mind than most people—especially in the sciences. Don't you think it's the height of hubris to believe you're the only world, the only people, in the entire galaxy of existence? Doesn't that belief seem more absurd than the reality of many worlds?"

I've never talked about it in professional circles—for obvious reasons—but it's long been a wondering of mine. What else—who else—is out there. But this... this is just... "Many worlds?"

He nods and leads me down a path lined with trees hanging with glowing fruit. In the distance, what I assume is the main town is alive with lights, sound, smells. As we near the area I see scantily clad men and women, some with pointed ears and unusual hair color, dancing, drinking, laughing, eating. Indulging in all the carnal pleasures without any worry, it would seem. Anyone else might blush and look away at the spectacle before us, but I have been to cultures all over my own world and seen how different people live, cele-brate, worship, love. Bodies are bodies. Sex is sex. I'm not embarrassed by nudity or public displays.

"Is it not late in the evening?" I ask.

"It is. Or likely very early in the morning. Perhaps two or three in the morning, if going by your sense of time. My kingdom never sleeps, especially at night."

We come closer to the crowds as we head up the main walkway to the palace, and as the people see us, they begin to bow before returning to their festivities.

"You have returned, my Prince," a woman with green eyes

and matching hair says, cozying up to Dr. Vane. She wears nothing but a few silk scarves strategically tossed over her body. Her pointed ears are studded with gemstones and she gestures to a group of women in similar garments. "Care to join us?"

"As much as I'd love to, I have business to attend," Dr. Vane says. "Another time perhaps."

She sighs, pouting a lip, then returns to her friends.

I glance at the man I thought was a stuffy old archaeologist in wonder. "Prince?"

He nods. "Indeed. Dr. Vane is only one of my many identities in the Nine Worlds. Here I am Prince Dean, son of the former King Lucian, brother to the current King Fenris and brother-in-law to Queen Arianna Spero, Midnight Star of Avakiri."

There's a sadness when he speaks of his brother and sister-in-law, and I sense a story there, but I have too many other questions. That one will have to wait.

"So you're royalty. You have a kingdom, but you come to Earth to dig up bones?" This is stretching my credulity.

"Would you stop doing what you love if you became a princess?" he asks.

My mouth snaps shut, as I have no good response to that.

"I know you mistrust me, and you should. But not because I'm a vampire, though I understand your hesitation in that regard," he says.

In a rush, all my fear, anger and hatred come flooding back into my veins, like boiling lava. I allowed myself to be distracted by all the wonders of this new world, but he's still a monster. In fact—oh shit. "Are all these people vampires?" I ask, shuddering. Am I surrounded by my greatest enemies?

"No," he says, studying my face. "But many, if not most, are. There are Fae, of course. Those with the ears you saw. And there are Shade. Those who are both Fae and vampire."

29

Fae. He throws that word out so casually. Like, of course. Fae. Duh. My mind—however—is spinning. "You're right," I say. "I don't trust you. But it is because you are a vampire. A monster."

He raises an eyebrow as we pass the threshold of the palace. The two guards on duty salute with a bow as we pass them. "Monster? That seems a harsh term for someone you just met. Someone who saved your life, as I recall."

"You live on blood and kill to survive. What else would you call that but monster?"

"There is a lot you don't know," he says, his face turning hard. "About my kind, and about me."

I stop walking, crossing my arms over my chest. I might regret this, but… "Take me back to my world. I'm done here."

"There must be quite the battle going on in that beautiful, fiery head of yours. On the one hand, you must be dying to see more of this world, to learn more about all the things you know nothing about. You have a chance to learn about an ancient culture that's still alive! On the other hand, you clearly have suffered trauma at the hands of someone like me. Your responses are too ingrained, too triggered to be thoughtfully considered."

He pauses, waiting for me to say something, but I press my lips together, angry that he can read me so well.

His lip twitches into something of a smile. "Let me ask you something. Are you racist?"

The question is so out of left field I don't even know what to do with it except answer. "Um, I mean, no. I try not to be. I suppose we are all influenced by the racial tensions of the culture we are raised, but having traveled extensively and immersed myself in different cultures, I think I've done a better job than most of exposing my own internal biases and dealing with them."

He nods. "Would your feelings about a different race

change, if whatever trauma you experienced at the hands of a vampire, were done by the hands of someone from a different race instead? Would you hate that whole race for the crimes of one person?"

I suck in a breath, unable to exhale for the longest moment."That's an unfair comparison. Vampires aren't human. Their biological needs are antithetical to human life. They are inherently killers."

He chuckles. "Looking at human history, you could say the same of man. Your biggest wars and largest death tolls weren't triggered by monsters. They were triggered by humans. Men, mostly. Do you hate all men? All humans?"

He has me at an impasse, because of course I don't. I glare at him, frustrated at this line of questioning.

"Give my kind a chance," Dr. Vane says with a charming smile. "You might be surprised you don't know everything there is to know about vampires. Where one might kill, another might heal." He winks, reminding me again of the debt I owe him, then pulls a ring off his finger and places it into my hand. "Show this to any vampire in this realm, and they will see you home safely. You are not my prisoner. But if you stay, I can help you. Rather, we could help each other." And with that, he walks away, letting me choose whether to follow or stay.

I stare at the ring in my palm. It's thick and gold, set with a blood red gemstone. The sides are etched with an ancient script I don't recognize. I slip the ring onto my middle finger, and consider my options.

Stay… or go.

He left the choice to me.

Making me culpable in my own destiny.

If I leave, I'll never know what he knows about the artifact I seek. Not to mention, I'll lose my chance to learn about this world and culture.

If I stay, I'll be sleeping with the enemy, so to speak. I will be putting my life at risk. And there are things on Earth I need to tend to.

In the end, there was never really a decision for me. I am who I am.

And so I follow the vampire into his lair.

DEAN VANE, PRINCE OF LUST

I knew she would follow, of course. What else could she do? Her mind is buzzing with curiosity and a quest for knowledge and understanding I have never seen in another person aside from myself. I feel pulled to her in a way that is unnerving for one such as myself. Usually, it is my pull over others that is the overwhelming force. And though I can smell her attraction to me, reluctant though it may be, it is not what one would expect. My draw to her is much stronger, putting us at an uncomfortable imbalance.

At least it's uncomfortable for me. She seems fairly oblivious to it, which makes the situation even more frustrating.

I knew Dr. Stone would be someone to contend with, though I had assumed she was a he, given the reports I'd received. Clearly she has done a good job of keeping her identity secret, though the 'why' of that is a curiosity I intend to sort out. I didn't expect her to be so knowledgeable of the paranormal—for a human at any rate. Though whether she is human or not is still up for debate, despite what she might say—or even believe—about herself. What she did with the Mother Tree, that shouldn't have been possible.

She's something extraordinary, and I'm going to need her to stop what I fear is coming—and to find my brother.

Whether she knows it or not, she might be the key to it all.

But first, she must learn to trust me, at least a little. Whatever a vampire did to her, it was bad. I can feel the hate coming off her in waves. It's almost painful.

I have a three-pronged strategy for building trust. First, a bath and food. Second, dazzle her with my collection of old books and artifacts. This strategy doesn't work with all women, but my gut says it will be immensely effective with this particular woman. And third, turn on the charm. I'd typically be a lot more optimistic about that third part, but with Dr. Alex Stone... well, let's just say I'm reserving judgment. If all else fails, I will show her the truth, if she's ready to see it.

"This way, Dr. Stone." I lead her through the palace and watch as her eyes widen at the splendid decor. The crystal, the tapestries, the original artwork dating back thousands of years, all of it would be wasted on anyone else. They would see the glamour of it all but wouldn't know the true worth. But I see in her eyes, she does.

She stops as we wind down a hall, her hand hovering over a crude figurine just over 11 centimeters tall. It is of a woman heavy with breasts, stylized in the extremities and face, made of oolitic limestone and tinted with red ochre. "Is this? It can't be. Is this the original Venus of Willendorf?" She looks at me, mouth agape.

"It is," I say, knowing there will be more questions. I wait for her to ask them.

"But how? It's supposed to be in a museum in Austria."

"That is also true. There were two figurines found in the dig in 1908. The one in the museum, and this one."

She shakes her head, disbelieving. "That's impossible."

"I assure you it's very possible. You see, I was there. I was the one who discovered them. In exchange for my particular talents, I was allowed to keep one."

"Bullshit," she says, her eyes still glued to the figurine. "Johann Veran, a workman, found it."

"My dear, human history is painfully easy to tweak. Your kind has such short memories and such greedy hearts. Enough money in the right hands, and anything you want can be reported as the truth. You can pick it up if you'd like," I say, knowing she's dying to.

She carefully removes it from its pedestal, cradling it carefully in her hands. Her eyes close, and a hum of magic pulses around her, the way it did when she touched the Mother Tree. Interesting. When she opens her eyes, the mistrust is gone, and a new accusation forms. With a sigh of regret, she places the figurine down. "It belongs in a museum," she says with judgment. But there's a trace of longing still there.

"Says who?" I ask, as we continue down the hall. "Who gets to decide what artifacts are meant for public display? Who chooses what pieces of history get ripped from their roots and tossed into museums? It smacks of white privilege, and usually only benefits western countries, leaving those places where art and artifacts are torn from none the better. It's colonialism at its finest, masked as service to the public." To be fair, I'm not anti-museum, but I have seen the abuses perpetrated by the system enough that I do not feel the least bit of guilt keeping pieces that wouldn't have been found otherwise.

She shakes her head, making no reply.

It's just as well, as we have arrived at her room. I open the door and gesture for her to enter. "Help yourself to anything you need. A servant will be here soon to help you get settled.

There's a bath ready for you, and clean clothes when you're done."

The fire is crackling in the hearth, and I made sure that every detail of her room would be perfect. The softest sheets and blankets, the plushest pillows, a variety of clothing styles in her size, oils, dried flowers and scented soaps at her disposal. No need left unattended.

She looks around the room and then frowns. "How did you know I would be coming here?"

"I assumed you would need somewhere to refresh after you healed in the grove, so I sent my staff ahead to prepare your room."

"I noticed there are no mirrors in here, or anywhere else in the palace."

"Indeed. Mirrors are forbidden for security reasons," I say.

"You're going to need to give more of an explanation than that," she says. "Is it some kind of bad luck mojo or?"

"It's how we traveled here from your world," I say. "For vampires, mirrors are portals. Doorways. It's why we can't see ourselves in them."

Her jaw drops. "Really? How fascinating."

A knock at the door interrupts us as an older Fae walks in carrying towels. "Forgive me, my Lord, but I wanted to make sure the towels were warmed before bringing them up."

I smile. "Helda, this is Dr. Alex Stone. She will be our guest for as long as she's willing to stay. Dr. Stone, this is Helda, one of my most faithful servants."

Dr. Stone frowns, then holds out her hand. "Helda, you can call me Alex."

Helda smiles, using her free hand to shake Alex's. "It's a pleasure to meet you, my dear. You're not the usual type the prince brings home."

I cough and glare at Helda, but she gives no mind to me,

and Alex laughs. It's the first time I think I've seen her really laugh, and it does something to me that I don't want to think too hard about just now.

Helda notices, though, as she tends to notice everything, and she raises an eyebrow. "I'll leave you two alone. Just ring the bell if you need anything, dear. I'll be up here in a flash. This is a big place, and folks have been known to get lost in the halls, so don't hesitate to call me."

"Thank you, Helda. I appreciate it."

Helda leaves the towels on the bed and walks out, closing the door behind her.

"Is she a slave or a paid servant?" Alex asks directly, as soon as Helda is gone.

"Paid servant. My brother and sister-in-law outlawed slavery over 100 years ago."

She exhales in relief. "Good."

I study the woman before me curiously. "You seem more impressed with my artifacts than with servants and plush extravagance."

"Is there a question in there?" she asks.

"It's implied," I say dryly.

"I'm used to wealth," she says. "It's just another kind of prison, a gilded cage, if you let it matter too much."

"May I ask how an archaeologist has acquired so much wealth?"

She sighs, as if tired of answering this question. "I've made my own share of money with books and such. But most of it is from my parents. My father was Robert Alexander."

And then it all clicks. "The famous movie star? He and his wife, the archeologist Dr. Sandra Stone, were murdered in their mansion nearly—"

"Fifteen years ago," she finishes, her face pale, her blue eyes fierce. "The only witness was their twelve-year-old daughter, who was left alive. She told the authorities what happened, that a monster drained her parent's blood and left them for dead, but no one believed her. 'A robbery gone bad,' they all said. Only nothing was stolen. Because the vampire didn't find what he was looking for. Or he did, and it was my parents."

No wonder she hates my kind. This might be harder than I initially thought. But the stakes are too high to give up. She must see reason, even if it's painful. And maybe, just maybe, there's a way I can help sweeten the pot for her. But that's a conversation for after she's refreshed.

"I'm sorry," I say, though the words are entirely inadequate. "I can't imagine what that must have been like for you."

"No," she says, crosses her arms again, a classic defensive posture. "You can't."

She's going to be a hard shell to crack, but the fate of all the worlds might be at stake, so this isn't something I can fail at. "I'll leave you to bathe. When you're ready, call for Helda, and she'll bring you to the dining room to eat."

She nods and I leave her, closing the door after me.

I head to my personal quarters—a large wing of the palace that contains my study, bedroom and private living quarters— the fatigue of the last few days weighing on me. When traveling to a new dig, I can't use a mirror. I can only use one upon leaving, when I know where I'm going. I do have hidden mirrors throughout the world, but eventually, I'm always required to travel over the desert for at least a few days. And I can't face the human sun. It makes this line of work challenging. And dangerous. But so rewarding I wouldn't dream of giving it up. Still, I need nourishment to replenish my strength for what is to come.

I ring a bell and within a few minutes, Helda arrives with a goblet. "This is fresh from Earth," she says, handing it to me.

I nod, thanking her. Before she leaves, she pauses at the door. "She's special, that one."

I don't have to ask who she's speaking of. "I know."

"Protect her."

Helda leaves before I can reply that I'm trying my best to do just that.

I take a long drink of the crimson liquid, quenching my thirst. At the queen's insistence, we've set up a humane trading system with our contacts on Earth. They find blood donors who are paid generously for their sacrifice. Blood is sent to us. We send money and unique goods only found in this world. No humans are harmed in the feeding and caring of the local vampires. Each vampire is allocated enough free blood to survive, with a thriving market if one wants to buy more. Everyone is happy.

Well, they should be.

But vampires, like humans, were not built to enjoy happiness for long. Our kind will always find something to create conflict over.

And with the king still missing, and the queen not quite herself from the recent curse cast on her by her own daughter, Inferna is in peril.

Losing Princess Aya hit this kingdom hard and hurt Avakiri, the Fae kingdom. Most assumed the princess would be the next Midnight Star, though that would be a long time coming, if ever, since Ari would have to die first.

My feelings for Arianna Spero have changed over the years. My desires for her have turned to brotherly affection, but my love for her is no less true. She is family, and her pain is my pain.

But I cannot save this kingdom. Asher will have to lead that venture. I'm more worried about saving the worlds.

I haven't shared my findings with my brothers, or with Ari. They are dealing with too much as it is.

But if my fears are confirmed, we are facing an even greater threat than the release of the Storm Spirit that tore holes in the fabric between worlds and destroyed parts of our kingdom and Avakiri.

Let's just hope that the illustrious Dr. Alex Stone clear herself of her prejudice long enough to help. Because all the lines of inquiry I track all lead back to her.

ALEX STONE

I allow myself the indulgence of a steaming bath in a stone tub as I scrub weeks of travel off my body. I seem to have taken most of the dessert with me, and I'm happy to see the true color of my skin again as I emerge from the washroom, smelling of rose oil. My own clothes are not only filthy, but wrecked from water, sun and knife damage, so I search the wardrobe for something clean to wear as a freshly stoked fire blazes in the hearth near my bed.

I'm still having a hard time fathoming that I'm in a new world, in the castle of a prince. It's all a bit surreal. But I approach this like any other expedition. There's a new culture to study, new rules to learn… this is my job. This is what I've trained so many years for.

But first, I need to get dressed. I'm hoping to find jeans. Something comfortable. But all I see are beautiful silk gowns in a variety of colors. I guess they dress for dinner here. I sigh and choose the black floor-length gown accented with what look like tiny chains that give the gown a gothic touch. Seems fitting. There are no mirrors in which to check myself, which is hard to get used to, but I improvise with some water in a bowl. My hair is easy enough, being short and straight, and I don't have any makeup to worry up.

I slide on matching slippers that feel like walking on clouds, and then ring the bell for Helda.

She arrives faster than seems possible, given the size of this castle, and I wonder if she has supernatural powers of speed, or was waiting for me in the halls, knowing I'd need her. Either way, I'm impressed.

Her smile is genuine when she greets me. "The prince is looking forward to dining with you," she says, guiding me out of the room and down the halls.

"What's he like?" I ask, wondering if she'll give me an honest evaluation of her employer, but knowing enough to take her words with a grain of salt.

"Prince Dean is… " she pauses, thinking, as we pass door upon door and my mind wanders, wondering what secrets hide within the rooms. Probably just more bedrooms.

"He is an enigma," she says. "His charm and charisma are powerful, and thus he gets a certain reputation. But there is more to him than meets the eye. Give him a chance." She looks over at me, her Fae ears pointing through the buns on her head, her face unlined but with a quality to her eyes that make me think she's much older than she appears.

When we arrive at the dining room, Dean stands, dressed in black formal wear that suspiciously compliments my gown nicely. The table is decked out in a lavish spread of food, which is a bit obscene if all of that is just for the two of us. He pulls out a chair at the head of the table and gestures for me to join him.

When we are both seated, his eyes land on mine. "You look beautiful," he says.

"Thank you." Changing the subject, I admire the food. "I

hope you plan on sharing this with your staff when we're done. This is a lot for just us."

"No worries. None of it will be wasted. Enjoy. You must be famished."

My stomach rumbles loudly as if on cue, but I do not turn away in embarrassment. It's perfectly normal to feel hunger after going so long without eating. "I guess I am," I say with a laugh, and I fill my plate with bits of everything.

We eat in silence. Partly because I'm too busy consuming everything in sight to carry on a conversation. Partly because I don't know what to say.

He's a perfect gentleman, and doesn't press me with questions or conversation until the food is removed and we are left with after dinner cocktails. "There's something I'd like to show you, if you'll join me?" he asks, standing.

I nod and follow him, the goblet of glowing blue liquor in my hand. I sniff it and find that it smells like cotton candy. My mouth waters, but I wait to taste it, unsure of how it will make me feel.

All thoughts of the drink are forgotten when we step into a room that you wouldn't even know is there at first glance. We enter through a tapestry hanging on the wall to find a room covered in shelves lining every wall filled with ancient books and scrolls and even more ancient artifacts from around the world. There's not a speck of dust anywhere, which tells me this is a room he spends a lot of time in and cares for.

In one corner is a large desk with parchment, an inkwell and a feather pen covering it. In the center of the room are two chairs upholstered in dark brown suede facing a matching love seat with a fireplace to the right. The walls are tall, spanning three stories, with walkways at each level and ladders on rollers positioned throughout.

KARPOV KINRADE

A guard stands at attention, blending into the shadows near the entrance, startling me as I turn and notice him.

He's a young man, or looks it. It's impossible to tell with vampires I suppose. But as I near him his eyes widen and his nostrils flare. My skin tingles, but I am pulled from his attention by the wealth of history stacked around me. "This is magnificent," I say, my eyes wide as I take it all in.

"I'm glad you like it."

He sits in the loveseat and watches me with a bemused expression as I explore the wonders that exist in this room. I could write a hundred dissertations on just one shelf of his collections. It boggles the mind. "You have pieces here that are only rumored to exist. They should be in museums," I reiterate, my former resentment stirring up again. It's not that he doesn't have a point, but most museums do their best to avoid the unethical collection of pieces and turn over things they discover have been unlawfully obtained. They serve to educate and inform the public about our history and other cultures. They are important, even if flawed.

He just smirks and sips from his drink.

When I've filled my head with everything I can, I sit across from him in one of the chairs, placing my drink next to me on a table. "So what now?" I ask.

"Cutting to the chase, I see," he says with a grin that exposes his dimples and makes his blue eyes light up. My god the man really is the most stunning creature I've ever seen.

I force myself to look away, to break eye contact before he sucks me into a spell I can't escape from. I notice my untouched drink with relief and reach for it, avoiding Dean and his inescapable pull. I take a long swig of it, delighting in the play of flavors dancing on my tongue, as an icy hot sensation coats my throat and stomach and settles into my blood and bones, making everything feel more relaxed.

"I'm not on holiday," I remind him, composing myself.

"I'm on a job. You said we could help each other. What did you have in mind?"

He nods, uncrossing his legs, and stands. "Very well. Let me show you." He walks across the room to his desk and reaches into a space that looks empty. There's nothing there, but his hand lands on something that he pulls out. As he does, a secret drawer appears.

"Neat trick," I say, trying to suss out the magic behind this.

He nods his head. "An easy way to keep secrets hidden."

"And yet *I* now know your secret," I say.

"You *are* one of my secrets," he says, holding eyes with me until I feel the weight of his gaze in my marrow. My pulse increases and skin flushes. A tingle of electricity runs up my spine and my head fills with thoughts of him. Of me. Of the two of us entangled under the moonlight, bodies joining together in ecstasy. This time he breaks the connection first, releasing me to breathe again.

I suck in air, crossing my arms over my chest and shivering at how intense that experience was. I find my voice, but it feels far away and pinched. "I don't understand."

He pulls a black velvet bag out of the hidden drawer and walks back, gesturing for me to join him on the loveseat.

I tip my goblet to my lips and drain the remnants of the blue liquid before sitting next to him. Our thighs brush together and a thrill of pleasure rushes up my leg, stealing my breath once again.

My visceral response to him makes me angry as it overlaps with my memories of the night my parents died. Maybe it's unreasonable. Maybe I need to have an open mind. But the trauma lives in my blood and in my gut and I can't make it disappear with wishful thinking or noble intent, so I sit with both emotions warring within me as he uses his long, elegant fingers to pull something out of the velvet bag.

I gasp when I see what he holds in his hand. A gently curved cream white stone that pulses with a preternatural light. He places it in my hand, and if there had been any doubts at all about its authenticity, they are gone.

I feel into the artifact, seeing its history, seeing how it would fit together perfectly with the piece I found in Israel and subsequently lost to my traitorous partner. "How do you have this?" I ask.

"It came into my possession about twenty years ago. A piece of the Fallen Star of Nirandel. Do you know the legend?"

I shake my head, transfixed. I never knew the name. Only heard the rumors of its power and that important men wanted it found. I've had my own reasons for hunting these pieces.

"Nirandel is one of the Nine Worlds, some say it's the original world of the dragons, the birthplace of the Ancient Ones who went on to create the other eight worlds and all who dwell upon them. In Nirandel, their stars are not like the stars of earth. They are special, and they almost never fall. When they fall on their own world, they are harvested with great care and made into sacred objects of power that are protected and used only by those who have the deepest respect for the power they wield. This is the first star to have fallen, at least in part, onto earth, and no one knows why. Every Star of Nirandel that falls is unique and possess its own special properties. This one is an ancient star, but has only been seen or talked about relatively recently. Many speculate as to what its powers are, but none know for certain. Not until the star is reformed with all its pieces."

My throat tightens, because I know what dark powers this star will possess once it's complete. I know it's a very bad idea. I'm just not sure if I can trust the man next to me enough to give him such dangerous knowledge.

I hand back his shard. "So there are other worlds, then. Besides this one and earth."

He nods.

"Have you been to them all?"

"No. Some aren't inhabitable. But I've been to most."

The things he must have seen. For a moment I have a twinge of jealousy at his life, at the artifacts he's collected and places he's seen. The history he's lived through. But none of that is worth sacrificing your soul for, I have to remind myself.

He places the shard back into the velvet bag. "I have one. You had one, which is now probably in the hands of Global Tech. I'm guessing by its shape, that leaves two more."

I nod. "Yes. There are four pieces," I confirm, shifting my eyes so he doesn't see the other truth I withhold from him. I stand, walking around the room again, avoiding eye contact with the prince. "We can't let Global Tech get their hands on any more of the pieces, and we have to get back from them what they have."

"We?" Dean says, a flirtation in his voice.

I sigh. "You know what I mean. This artifact has power, even in its current form. Too much power." I can feel it under my skin, even now, even without touching it, pulsing, vibrating with energy begging to be used. And I know what it can do. The temptation to wield this power would be too great for anyone. Even me. Maybe especially me.

To distract myself from dark thoughts, I let my hand glance over the shelves of history, closing my eyes as I soak in the stories each piece tells. I'm learning more about his world, and my own, in these few minutes of discovery, than I have in years of excavations, and it humbles me and pulls at an ache in my chest. Towards the end of one shelf, tucked in the back behind a grimoire, I notice a shallow bowl, simple in design, filled with water. I wander towards it as if pulled by a magnetic force. As I stare into the water, forms appear in the reflection, and then, I am swept away by the visions that consume my mind.

I'm home, in our expansive dining room, sitting at the table, smiling. I'm an adult, much the same as I am now, only both of my parents are present. My dad is flipping pancakes and making a joke about penguins, and my mom is cutting fresh fruit. He leans over to kiss her head as they work together in tandem, their orbits connected, their bodies in sync. They're older than I remember. My father has graying temples and they both hold deeper laugh lines and a few new worry lines. I watch as they move as one, my heart full. I've never been this happy, not since I was a child. The sun is covering the world in a spray of orange and red hues and the smell of the ocean wafts in from the open windows that overlook a view to die for. But my eyes are stuck on my parents. Alive. Happy. In love. And with me. My dad serves the pancakes and my mom places a bowl of fruit on the table. They join me and we eat together, sharing stories about our day, our work, our plans. My mom and I have a dig together, one my dad will be joining in between movie shoots. My heart is near bursting with joy, and I know I can happily stay in this reality forever. This is what my life was meant to be like. This is where I must stay.

I help clean up after breakfast and my father sits at our grand piano to play a tune while my mother sings and laughs. I join in, catching the melody, though I didn't inherit my mother's melodious voice.

Then I hear my name being called from a great distance, as if through water.

"Alex! Alex!"

The voice becomes more urgent, and I look around, wondering where I am. The scene with my parents fades, the room disappearing, their smiles turning to smoke as a new face materializes before me. Dean Vane, with worried blue eyes, stands inches from me, his mouth turned down, his brow furrowed. "Alex, come back to me."

I stumble and he catches me, as the reality crashes into my heart. "What was that?"

He holds me steady and peers at the bowl of water. "That's the Mirror of Idis. It shows us what might be, if things were different. It can be very hard to resist losing yourself in its visions."

"No shit," I say with a painful laugh.

"What did you see?" he asks, tilting his head.

"My parents. I saw my parents." My hands grip his arms tightly, and I feel a certainty surge within me. "We have to destroy the shards of the Fallen Star of Nirandel," I say. "They are too dangerous for anyone to ever collect for themselves."

Because I know what I would do with them if I could wield that power, and it would take everything in me to stop myself from committing a great evil with that artifact.

As we turn to exit the room, we pass the man who has been quietly acting as a sentinel. I didn't look closely at him before, but now I see that his eyes are wide and he looks pained.

With a groan, he throws himself at me, sword in hand, teeth elongated, a primal growl rising from his throat.

His teeth sink into my neck before I know what's happened, and I kick and punch but he is armored and has a weapon pinned into my gut as he feeds on my blood. Pain permeates everything in me and my vision swims. Another roar fills my ears, and the guard is pulled away. My body falls like a limp rag doll to the floor as Dean tears into the man, his normally handsome face distorted by rage as he ends the vampire's life with a quick twist of his neck.

He rushes back to me, the bloodlust in him fading as he

sees my state. "I'm so sorry. That should have never happened."

But of course it should have. I am, after all, surrounded by monsters. I was stupid to let my guard down because of a pretty face and nice words. These creatures are deadly, and I am only food to them.

ALEX STONE

J'm shaking, more in rage than pain, though there's plenty of both to go around, as Dean escorts me out of the room and through the halls. We head back to the dining room, where he sits me down and proceeds to give commands to everyone near him. He's pissed, clearly, but also worried.

"I can offer you my blood," he says, the normal bluster and confidence in his eyes gone. "It will heal you quickly."

I glare at him. "Nope. I'm good."

He nods and grabs a napkin from the table, pressing it to my neck to stem the bleeding. "It is rare for a vampire to lose control like that, but it does happen. Normally they are sent to a special island, to keep others safe and give them a chance to gain control of themselves. We don't get a lot of humans here. But even so, this isn't what most of us are like."

"Really?" I ask, my skepticism clear. "Because it seems to me this is par for the course. I never should have stayed. I want to go home now." My voice is firm, only belied by the vague dizziness I'm still feeling from the attack, and the experience of seeing my parents, of living a reality that will never be. Of knowing once and for all what's actually at stake.

"Let's get you fixed up and then I'll take you home, if that's what you want."

"It is," I say, a little less firmly than before. The man is arrogant and cocky and infuriating, but right now he's being compassionate and kind and it's a lot harder to stay mad at him like this. Still, he's no different from the monster that killed my parents and the one that just attacked me.

I steel myself against any softening of my nerves as Helda joins us, a small jar of ointment in her hands.

She passes it to Dean, giving him a chastising look, before turning her attention to me. "This isn't the best introduction to Inferna you could have gotten, but it's not all bad, my dear."

I don't know what to say to the kindly Fae, so I hold my tongue as Dean removes the napkin and applies the ointment to the wound. His fingers are cool and gentle and the touch sends an unwanted shiver up my spine. Damn this man.

"This will heal you," he says. "It will just take a bit longer than my blood would have. And might leave a small scar."

"What's in it?" I ask. I sniff and detect hints of lavender, but the other scents are foreign to me, though it's vaguely similar to my friend's concoctions that have saved my skin—literally—more than once.

He shrugs. "It's an ancient Fae mixture. They don't share their secrets with vampires."

"Smart."

Helda snorts in laughter and turns to walk away, but not before giving Dean another look of disappointment. He shifts his eyes away from her piercing glance and focuses back on my neck. Once the ointment is applied, he covers it with a bandage and leans back. "You're all set. But… are you sure? There's so much at stake, and everything I've learned has me convinced we have to work together. There are pieces to the puzzle neither of us are seeing yet."

I sigh, exhausted and frustrated. "There is no 'us.' I... I appreciate you saving my life back in Israel. But being with you, being here... it puts me at greater risk. Vampires aren't safe. They never have been. Nothing I've seen so far has changed my mind about that." I place a hand over the bandage, a low ache forming as the ointment presumably gets to work healing the skin. "I'll find the other pieces on my own and stop Global Tech. You should destroy the one you have."

He raises an eyebrow. "How do you propose I do that?" he asks.

"I—" my voice stalls as I realize I honestly have no clue. "The fires of Mordor?" The joke slips from my mouth before I can hold it in, and his eyes sparkle in amusement as he chuckles. I can't help but laugh too, whether at my joke or the absurdity of it all I don't rightly know.

I'm not usually so angry and mistrusting, though given recent events maybe I should be a tad more cautious about the men in my life. I know, understatement of the year, right?

"I don't know how to destroy the artifact," I admit. "That's not a secret it's anxious to give up to me."

Dean leans back, thinking. "I've tried to destroy it," he says, surprising me.

"Why?" For a man who collects precious things, that would be the ultimate sacrilege. Even for me, knowing what I know, it's hard to fathom destroying something with so much history.

"From the things I've learned about the Stars of Nirandel, it seemed the safest course. Their powers become corrupted on other worlds, particularly on earth. Even on their world, the stars are misused, despite how religiously they are guarded. It has caused abnormalities in their powers, deviations in their genetics, and war amongst their people. And this is a power inherent to their world. I assumed that on earth, the power would be even more damaging, and I've seen what unbridled power can do. I don't know all the secrets of this artifact, but I know enough to make me very cautious."

"What have you tried?" I ask, tucking all this information away in my mind.

"The usual," he says. "Fire, magic, spells. Nothing worked. If anything, it seemed to grow stronger, absorbing the power."

"Interesting," I say, considering what that could mean. "Is it possible that it can't be destroyed at all?"

He shrugs. "Everything can be destroyed. You just need to find its weakness."

A scream interrupts our conversation as a guard explodes into the dining room. "Prince Dean, the artifact room has been breached."

We both stand at the same time, likely with the same thought. "The star fragment," I say under my breath.

"Wait here," he commands, running out of the room with his guard.

"Yeah, I'm not a 'wait here' kind of woman," I say, looking for anything that can be used as a weapon and choosing a steak knife from the table before retracing my steps towards the secret room.

My mind spins with the possibilities as I approach. Did Global Tech track us down? How did they get to another world, though? There are too many unanswered questions as I move to catch up to Dean and his guards.

I hear shouting, then the sound of a body hitting the wall with a wet thud. I run faster, my knife at the ready. I'm no warrior, but I've been in a fair amount of scuffles with supernatural horrors. I can hold my own, though I usually prefer my ice axe to a dinner knife. It's more effective in cleaving monster skulls.

The lights are out in the halls, and I'm forced to navigate in near pitch darkness. My night vision hasn't kicked in when I stumble over a body and nearly impale myself on my own weapon. That would have been a way to go. Nice job, Alex. Scrambling up, my head still a bit wobbly from the blood loss and adrenaline rush, I'm not at my best.

Still, nothing could have prepared me for what I see when I pull back the tapestry and enter the room.

Bodies litter the floor.

Dean is leaning against a wall holding his gut as blood pours over his hands. His face is more ghastly pale than ever, his eyes pained and shocked in equal measure.

In the center of the bodies stands a woman holding Dean's piece of the Star. At her hip is a belt with the other piece dangling from it. The piece I excavated in Israel.

She's got long brown hair the color of chestnuts, soft hazel eyes, and hasn't aged a day in fifteen years.

My knife falls to the ground, my jaw slack, my mind not believing what I'm seeing.

The blood splattered creature stealing from us is…

My mother.

I step forward, dumbstruck, unsure of what to say or do. Nothing makes sense. Nothing.

"You died," I say, my eyes filling with tears.

Her attention flicks to me, and as the bloodlust in her wanes, I see a glimpse of the woman she used to be. The woman who raised me, who read me stories and gave me baths and always made time to have tea with me and my stuffed animals.

I don't know how to reconcile what I'm seeing with my memories, and so I stand, stunned, unable to move.

"I'm sorry, Alex," she says, her voice the same one from

memories, with the lilting British accent. Before I know what's happening, she pulls a mirror from her pocket and then she's gone, as if she was never there.

The small mirror falls to the ground, shattering into pieces.

ALEX STONE

*D*ean's moans snap me from my temporary paralysis. I rush to him and offer support, but his body is dead weight as I practically drag him to the couch. He can't walk and can barely move. I'm fairly certain he's actually holding in his intestines, from the looks of that slash across his abdomen. It doesn't bode well.

All the guards are dead. We are in a remote part of the castle. I'm at a loss.

His breathing slows. I don't really know what kills vampires. Lore would say this isn't enough, but how accurate is that? I've got no clue. Can they really live with their guts spilling out of them?

So I have a choice…

Let him die.

Or feed him my blood.

I assume that part of lore is correct. My blood should help. And he did the same for me.

It's the right thing to do. I think.

Suddenly everything I thought I knew about the who's

good and who's bad has been flipped on its head, and I feel as if I know nothing. As if my whole world has been a lie.

But I don't have time to second guess myself. Or rather, Dean doesn't have time for me to be indecisive. Whether this wound will kill him or not, he must be in agony.

I scramble across the room, knocking into bodies as I search for the knife I dropped earlier. I find it wedged between the dismembered head of a guard and a bookshelf. Lovely. Shaking like one of those chihuahuas who never seem to calm down, I make my way back to Dean and steady my hand as I slide the knife over the soft fleshy part of my forearm. The cut stings as blood begins to trickle out of the wound. I hold it over his mouth and will him better.

Blood spills onto his lips, casting crimson splatters onto his deathly pale skin. It takes a moment for him to respond. I lower my arm to his mouth and in a violent burst of life his lips seek my blood, his teeth elongating as they find purchase in my flesh, and he begin to drink deeply.

Heat burns through my arm and travels through my body. It's not unpleasant, but rather intoxicating. I begin to feel sleepy as he drinks more and more from me, until I cannot keep my eyes open any longer.

When darkness takes me, I go to it willingly.

* * *

I EXPECTED NIGHTMARES, but my sleep was a dreamless one. When I wake, I am dressed in a silk nightgown and laying under fur blankets with a fire warming the room.

And I'm surprised to discover I'm not alone in the bed. As I shift, I feel the body of a man, his skin cool, his muscles firm. He is naked from the waist up and when I open my eyes in the dimness of the room, he is propped on his side staring at me.

58

"Did you sleep well?" Dean asks.

I try to sit up, but my body feels made of led and so I stay where I'm at, enjoying the flames dancing on the walls and warmth of the bed. Even the prince's body next to mine offers a kind of comfort I didn't expect. "I'm still tired," I say, yawning.

"You lost a lot of blood, but you saved my life." He looks at me quizzically. "You're an enigma, Dr. Stone. You hate my kind, yet you risked your life to save me. Why?"

Our faces are inches apart, and as I awaken, so does my body. Need for him grows in me, as old prejudices are replaced by new truths. "You were right," I say. "I was judging an entire race based on one man's evil deeds. You've been kind when I wasn't. You saved my life and offered me your trust. If you weren't a vampire I wouldn't have held the same prejudice. I was nearly killed and left for dead by a human. I was saved by a vampire. My whole life feels like it's been turned upside down."

He lifts a hand and traces my face with the pad of his finger, and I sigh at the contact as my nerve endings come alive. Whatever my mind has thought of the sexy prince, my body has clearly had its own ideas and is ready to act on them.

"How did we end up in bed together?" I ask, my own nervous energy evident in my voice.

"Helda wanted to keep an eye on both of us," he says, his eyes locked on mine, his finger moving down my chin to my throat. "She found us after you passed out. She stayed with us until I woke and relieved her. It took some convincing, but she finally left about an hour ago."

"You've just been watching me sleep for an hour?" I ask, my voice catching in my throat.

"You look at peace when you sleep," he says. "I find it mesmerizing."

His face is inches from mine. I can feel his breath against my skin, his body pressed against mine, and I know my blood has healed him better and faster than I could have expected. His abs have returned to their normal, ripped selves. His body is responding to our proximity with a clear message of desire.

I give into my own temptations and lift my hand to his waist. The contact sends shivers through us both, and he lowers his own hand from my neck to my chest, tracing the line of my nightgown just above my breasts. My breath shudders and fires light in me.

"Alex," he says, his voice a low rumble. "I don't know what you're doing to me, but if you want to stop, tell me soon."

Logic says I should stop.

But my body laughs at logic.

Instead, I take his hand in mine and lay it on my breast, then glide my own hand down his body until it catches the part of him that is clearly ready for more. "Don't stop," I say, breathless with anticipation.

My words trigger a wave of desire pulsing in both of us. His hand grips my ribs as he lowers his face, his lips finding mine. Our first kiss is an exercise in controlled passion as his tongue explores my mouth and his teeth nibble at my bottom lip.

My fingers dig into his back as he moves his body between my legs, pulling my nightgown up and over my head as he does. He still has silk bottoms on, but I'm now naked as his gaze lingers on my scar-riddled body.

He traces each one he finds, first with his fingers, then his tongue, making trails of lava-like heat all over my skin. "Tell me about these," he says, his voice thick with desire.

And so I tell him the stories of my body, of the tombs I've explored, the monsters I've fought, the times I've nearly died. As he moves down my body, my back arches in need and desire, and then I am gone, consumed by him, by his touch, by his kisses, by his exploration of me as if I am the only thing in his world that has ever mattered.

Words disappear along with his pants, and when we become one, the world around us disappears as well.

The power of our passion is not spent quickly, and the fire has died to embers by the time we fall into each other's arms in exhausted splendor.

For what feels like hours we do not talk, not with words, but we lay and enjoy each other's closeness for as long as we can.

We both know that our next steps will be perilous. That the journey we're on to recover the Fallen Star of Nirandel could be deadly.

And so we savor this moment, knowing it might be our last together.

As the sun rises, Helda comes to the door with food, blood, and juice. I pass on the blood, but am not as repulsed as I would have been seeing Dean drink it.

He explains to me their humane way of acquiring blood, and I'm impressed and humbled by their commitment to not harm humans.

"If time were not our enemy, I would spend an eternity in this room with you, showing you all the ways I desire to pleasure you," he says, once our food is consumed, and it's clear we have to get up.

His words bring promises too tempting to think on right now. There are more urgent matters to discuss, though my unquenchable body disagrees. "I have to tell you something," I say.

He sits up, listening.

"Last night, the woman who stole your piece of the star. That was my mother."

"So she must have been turned the night you thought she

was killed," he said, reaching that logical conclusion must faster than my addled brain did last night.

"That's my assumption," I say. "But why would she be doing this? You've shown me being a vampire doesn't inherently make you evil. My mother was a good person. The best I know. Why would she become a monster?" Saying the words brings up a well of emotion, and Dean pulls me in his arms. The warmth, the closeness, comforts me even as it scares me. This has happened so fast. It's insane. And yet, nothing feels more perfect than being with him.

"Power can make anyone mad, even the best of us," he says. "She had the other piece of the Star last night. It gave her power I've never seen. She tore through my men and me. Not a small feet for anyone. Now she has two and will be even more powerful."

I pull away, my heart racing at what I've just realized. "Three. She'll have three soon," I say.

"How so?"

"There's something I haven't told you. Something I didn't know if I could trust you with. I have my own piece of the Star. I always assumed it was what the vampire who killed my parents was after. It's what started me on this quest."

He frowns. "Where is it?"

"In a safe under my house in Malibu," I say.

"Does your mother know this?" he asks.

"She knows we have it. She found it, after all. But I built a new safe for it after a break-in several years ago, and she doesn't know about that."

He caresses my face, kisses me quickly, then takes leave of the bed. "We have to get to it. We can't let her get three pieces. She will be nearly unstoppable."

"Dean, I think I know why she wants it," I say, finally sharing my last secret with him.

He turns mid-way through dressing. "Why?"

"I know what it can do. What its power is." I swallow, my heart falling in my chest. "It can bring back the dead," I say. "Fully restored. As if they never died. If my father is actually dead, I think she wants to use it on him. It's what I would do."

He studies me. "How do you know this?"

"It's my ability," I say, realizing *this* is actually my last secret from him. "I can read the history of things. It's how I knew what the Mother Tree was feeling. And your blood, it unlocked more of that power in me. Now, I can see the web everyone walks in and how it all connects. I can see the patterns. I know this is what my mother is going to do."

"I knew you weren't human," he says. "Feeding on your blood confirmed it for me."

"I think you're right," I say. "But I don't know what I am." A mystery maybe my mother can help me resolve, now that I know she's alive. Of course, she's the villain now, so we'll see how that goes.

"Something so much more," he says, his voice a soft caress over my heart. Then his face darkens, and he frowns. "What's the cost?" he asks. "There's always a cost for this kind of magic."

"Innocent lives. So many innocent lives." My voice chokes with emotion. "My mother is willing to let hundreds of innocent people die to bring back my father. And the more the Star is used for this purpose, the hungrier it will get. In the wrong hands, it could result in an apocalypse like we've never seen."

Dean pulls some clothes out of his closet and tosses them to me. "Then we'd better get going and stop this before it's too late."

I dress quickly, though his clothes are too big for me. We are both silent, lost in our thoughts, but I can tell they run on parallel tracks.

We are both worried that it's already too late.

ALEX STONE

$\mathcal{D}$ean and I stand in front of a large mirror, ready to travel back to my world. I'm nervous. This just got so much more personal on so many levels.

"I can't take us directly to your house, since I haven't been there, but I can get us close."

I nod and take his hand, and he pulls us through. I obviously traveled this way once before, but I was unconscious so it hardly counts. My stomach drops as my body is sucked into a vortex of magic that dances all over my skin. It's a heady experience, as if traveling through galaxies, through a dark and starry night. Dean's hand grips mine firmly, and I cling to his, not wanting to get lost in this universal expanse of nothingness. The absence of any sound is the most disconcerting, like what I'd imagine being in space is like.

Moments later, or hours later, I can't really tell, we are sucked out of another mirror and into a covered alley lined with trash bins. The mirror we came from is a graffiti-covered attachment to a brick wall that forms the backside of a line of shops.

At least a dozen homeless are camped out around the

bins, using cardboard boxes and bits of cloth to form makeshift houses. You can't drive through Los Angeles without seeing camps of homeless people under overpasses and lining the streets. It breaks my heart, and I wish I knew a way of fixing this growing problem. I donate to organizations that I know work hard to help those less fortunate or privileged, but it never seems enough.

Dean shakes his head as we make our way through the web of bodies. "And people think we're the monsters. You'll never find anyone in my realm living like this," he says.

It's past dusk, the sun already a memory in the night sky as we walk down the street, and I orient myself to where we are as I search for a cab to take us to my house. "What would we have done if it was daylight?" I ask.

"Waited," he says, shrugging.

"Oh to have the patience of an immortal," I tease.

He winks at me and reaches for my hand, holding it as I hail a cab.

The intimate everyday gesture sends flurries of butterflies to my stomach, and I wonder how long we'll have this— whatever *this* is.

I tell him a bit more about my parents on the drive to my house. "They met in college. My mom was studying archaeology and anthropology and my dad was majoring in theater arts. It was love at first sight, to hear them tell it."

My cheeks warm as the prince studies me. "Sometimes that is the way of it," he says. "Two people who are meant to be often know instantly. As if their souls have danced the same dance before and they were only seeking each other for another round together."

"You believe in soul mates?" I ask.

He nods. "I do now."

The cab pulls into my driveway and I let his words settle into me as I pay electronically using PayPal. I don't have my wallet or phone, so I have to borrow the driver's cell. After setting up his payment, I send a text to my friend, letting her know we might need help if shit hits the fan here, then I hand the phone back with a thank you.

The cab speeds away as Dean and I face my house.

The prince whistles. "No wonder you weren't that impressed by my castle. You've got one of your very own."

He turns to admire the view of the ocean and mountains and then follows me to the front door. I don't have my key, but I had a thumbprint system installed just for these occasions.

As we enter, a familiar voice greets me in a deep British accent. "Good evening, Alex, you've been gone longer than expected. I modified your food delivery and cleaning service accordingly."

Dean startles, looking around. "Is someone here?"

I chuckle. "No, I had Smart House Technology installed a year ago. It's the house talking to us."

He shakes his head. "My brother, Ace, would love this place."

I grin. "He's welcome anytime." And I'm stunned at how fast I've come to accept Dean and his family of vampire brothers into my life. It's incredible how fast things can change.

I give him a quick tour of the place, showing off the dining room, kitchen, entertainment room and game room. We skip the many guest bedrooms, and I'm showing him the master bedroom that I sleep in when my house speaks again, and my heart stops cold. "Alex, you have a guest in the living room. She claims she is your mother."

"She's here," I say to Dean, stating the total obvious.

"I guess it's time I meet your mother properly," he says, holding out his hand.

I take it, and we make our way downstairs.

My mother is standing in front of the fireplace staring into the flames. She turns when we approach. "Darling, I've missed you so much."

She comes towards me, arms open, and I let go of Dean's hand to approach her. "Is it really you?"

"It is. I'm so sorry. For everything. I had no idea you were involved in this. I came here to explain."

She reaches for my hand and I let her. I don't feel the energy of the Star pieces on her, and don't see them anywhere. My eyes burn with unshed tears, too many emotions warring within me.

"You've become everything I imagined you would. Your father would be so proud of you," she says, her voice catching on emotion.

"So he's… he's really dead?" I know he is, but I need to hear her say it.

She nods. "I was saved that night, but he was too far gone."

"Why… why didn't you come back for me?" I search her eyes for lies, for truth, for understanding, something.

"It's complicated. At first, I couldn't control my thirst and didn't want to put you in danger. And I didn't think you would want me after I was turned into a monster. I thought you'd be better off without that in your life. Without me in your life." Her eyes spill over with tears and she lets them fall as she holds eye contact with me.

My heart breaks in that moment, and I pull her into a hug. "I needed you. I needed my mother."

All the pain and grief I felt for her for fifteen years swells up in me and breaks through my carefully manufactured walls. I pull back, looking at her again, not wanting to break contact, not wanting to lose her again, despite what I know of her, despite the truth that is gnawing away at the back of my mind. I know I shouldn't trust her. That she's murdered to get the Fallen Star of Nirandel and will do so again, but it's painfully difficult to align that knowledge with the fact that the mother I remember is right here, holding me. "I never thought I'd see you again."

She smiles through her tears. "We can be together now. Forever, if you want. We can be a real family."

My heart thumps in my chest. Because I know what's coming next, and I can't face it. It's too tempting. Too torturous. The Mirror of Idis showed me what might have been. But because of the power of the Star, it inadvertently showed me what still could be as well. If I'm willing to pay the price.

"I just need your piece of the Star, honey. Once we find the fourth piece, I can bring your father back, and everything can be as it should be."

I step away from her, and she frowns. "Darling, it's okay. I'm not going to hurt you. This star was brought into our lives for a reason. I can fix what happened to our family that night. I just need your help. With your powers, we can find the last piece and set right all we lost."

"Do you know what you're asking?" I take another step back, afraid I will be sucked into her desires, to her wants, to her needs, and that I will lose my sense of right. "Do you know what price the Star demands for use of its power?"

I want to believe she doesn't. That when she discovers the horror of the cost, of the lives that would be sacrificed, she will realize we could never use its power, not even to bring my father back. But I see on her face the truth. She already knows. And she doesn't care. She's willing to sacrifice innocent lives for her own selfish gain.

"I can't do what you're asking. I won't tell you where my piece is or help you find the final piece."

"Please, don't do this," she begs. "You don't know what you're doing. Who you're angering. Just… give me the shard and tell me where to find the last piece. I promise you won't be hurt."

I laugh, but there is no humor in it. "Do you think I'm worried about myself right now? Are you serious? What happened to every lesson you ever taught me as a child? To the difference between right and wrong? To self-sacrifice? To choosing the moral high ground even when it hurts? Where did the woman who taught me those lessons go? Do you really think Dad would want to be brought back if he knew the cost?"

Her eyes flick to something behind me, giving me only a moment to react before I realize we're not alone.

A figure appears as if from smoke, standing in the corner of my living room across from us. He is draped in a black robe and wears a black leather mask over half his face. The other half is sheer perfection. Blue eyes, pale white hair. And filled with cruelty. Around his waist is a chain with the two Star shards hanging from it.

He smiles maliciously, but only half his face responds.

Dean gasps, and I look at him as he stares at the man.

"Levi?" the prince says, clearly stunned. "What? How?"

The man, Levi, takes a step forward. "It's been a long time, brother."

"You're dead," Dean says, and it's a total Deja Vu. How many dead family member reunions are we going to have today, I wonder morbidly.

"You should know we Vane brothers aren't so easy to kill." Levi takes off his mask and reveals the other side of his face. It's as if someone melted off half his face. I cringe in disgust.

"I found a way to live, but not fully. I need the Fallen Star of Nirandel to complete my transformation, and your new girlfriend is going to help with that. If she doesn't, both you and her precious mommy will die."

DEAN VANE, PRINCE OF WAR

I cannot process what I'm seeing. My brother has been alive all these years? He died over 100 years ago during the war. How can this be? And yet, it is true. He stands here, in the flesh, taunting me.

And he wants to use Alex for his own gain. The power he already possesses is too great, especially for his warped mind.

"Don't help him," I tell her. "No matter what he does, do not give him access to the Star."

Levi flicks his wrist, and I am sent flying into the living room wall, crashing into the drywall. With a power he shouldn't have, he pins me in place, paralyzing me, squeezing my internal organs until I can't help but scream out in pain. I feel my life force being drained slowly from me, siphoned off by the power of the Star shards.

"Stop!" Alex rushes him, stupid, brave woman that she is, and with another flick of his wrist she's frozen in place, her face pained, her eyes wide.

"You promised you wouldn't hurt her," Alex's mother says.

"I'm not hurting her, just inspiring her to do what's in her best interest. And yours." Levi's eyes pierce through Sandra Stone. "Or have you forgotten our deal?" he asks.

And then it all clicks into place. Or most of it. "You turned Alex's mother, didn't you? After sending a vampire to retrieve their Star shard?"

"I needed her help to locate the others. I had no idea her daughter had the real power until much later."

Alex's eyes widen at this news, and she glares at her mother, who looks away, ashamed.

"You're helping the man who had my father killed?" Alex asks, as she struggles with the paralysis keeping her in place.

"It's more complicated than that," Sandra says. "Just do what he says. He won't hesitate to hurt you or those you love to get what he wants."

"Is that how he keeps control over you?" I ask Sandra. "By threatening Alex if you don't help and promising you your husband back if you do?"

Again she looks away, and I know I've hit in on the nose. My self-congratulation doesn't last long as Levi's limited patience wears thin. "This is a charming family reunion, but I'm not getting any younger," he says with some irony.

He walks over to Alex, and when he's a few inches from her, he grabs her hand and forces it onto the two Star shards he carries on the chain around his waist. "Tell me where yours is and where I can find the fourth one."

Alex squeezes her eyes shut, and I can see the internal struggle as she tries to resist Levi's control, but it's no use. He's stronger than us all at this point.

"Don't tell him!"

Alex shakes her head, pressing her mouth shut.

"She doesn't have to tell me, I can see what she sees," Levi says, sending a chill down my spine.

Tears stream down Alex's face, and I fight against Levi's restraints trying to reach her. The harder I fight, the weaker I become. After a few more moments, Alex collapses to the ground, and I can't tell if she's conscious or not. Levi smiles, the gloat clear on his half-deformed face. He looks to Sandra, who is frozen in place, her face an emotionless mask. "Your daughter's gifts have grown beyond what you told me. It's incredible. We will take her with us. She will be very useful."

He looks at me. "You, not so much. I have no further need of you, once I have the third shard."

At that, he looks to the mahogany wood floors and touches the Star shards, concentrating his powers until a beam of white light emanates from his hands and begins to burn a hole through the floor all the way to the basement. "Get it," he tells Sandra, once the hole is complete.

Without a word, she jumps into the hole, landing in a crouch on the basement floor. It doesn't take her long to find Alex's shard and return with it, handing it meekly over to Levi.

Alex still isn't moving or waking up. I can sense her pulse, but it's faint.

Once Levi has all three, he grins wickedly. "This is our final farewell, brother."

His hand glows, and he's about to aim it at me when lightning crashes through the windows and a giant silver manticore blasts into the living room. Atop the beast is a woman I recognize, but am stunned to see here.

Alex stirs, opening her eyes and sitting up. She smiles when she sees the woman on the manticore. "You came."

"Of course. Sorry I'm late. Who are we beating up today?" Iris, formerly First Hunter and now the youngest Watcher on the Council of Hunters, says as she faces Levi. "You, I'm guessing, based on the hideous face and lackluster attempt at sinister costuming. Theo, you know what to do!"

Theo blasts my brother with lightning bolts from his eyes,

hitting Levi in the chest. That should have been the end of him, but Levi screams and uses the power of the Star to protect himself and counterattack. The house around us shifts. The walls, ceiling and floor splinter as lightning and magic shoot everywhere, destroying the mansion while we're still in it.

"Come on kids, we've gotta get out of here," Iris says.

I help Alex up and onto Theo, mounting after her, and the manticore flies out of the living room window and into the night sky.

As we climb higher, Levi continues his attacks on us, singeing Theo's fur with blasts of magic.

"We need a door!" Iris says.

"What?" Alex asks, screaming to be heard.

"A door. Some kind of door."

We all look down, and I point to a row of houses. "Will one of those work?"

Iris nods and guides Theo down in a descent so fast I have to grip Alex to keep her from falling off.

We land with a heavy thud, and in an instant Theo shrinks to the size of a kitten and hops onto Iris' shoulder. She pulls an ancient key from a chain around her neck and sticks it into the front door keyhole of a stranger's house.

"Isn't this breaking and entering?" Alex asks, still wobbly on her feet from Levi's power over her.

"Just wait," Iris says with a wink.

When the door opens, we aren't in the expected stranger's house but rather we are in a familiar place to me.

"Oh my," Sly Devil says, seeing us appear in his study. "What kind of trouble have you brought me today, my dear niece?"

Iris shrugs. "This is my friend, the one I was telling you about," she says, gesturing to Alex, who is taking it all in. "And you know Dean, of course."

73

Sly winks. "Of course I know the Prince of Lust. I just didn't realize you three all knew each other."

Alex turns looking at us both. "I didn't either. How do you two know each other?"

"I was going to ask you the same thing," I say. "How do you know Iris? I know her because she's on the Hunter's Council and is engaged to my nephew."

Alex's eyes widen and Iris smiles and holds out her hand to show off the ring. Alex screeches. "You're engaged! Why didn't you tell me?"

Iris shrugs. "We've both been so busy. I posted it on Facebook."

Alex rolls her eyes. "I'm not on Facebook. You know that." Then Alex pulls the Watcher into a hug. "Congratulations. What's he like?"

Iris grins. "Sexy. Stubborn. Kind. You'll meet him eventually. First, tell me, what the blazes is going on?"

Sly clears his throat. "Ladies? Can we get to the part where you explain why you are all here looking like something the cat dragged in?"

I step forward. "Sly, this is Dr. Alex Stone, the key to finding the final pieces of the Fallen Star of Nirandel. My brother, Levi, didn't die in the war as we thought, and now has three of the four pieces. We have to find the last one before he does, or he could very well usher in the apocalypse for all nine worlds."

"I see. Well, that is something then, isn't it?" Sly says.

Alex steps forward. "I think I know where the final piece is, which means so does Levi."

"*I* had a vision," I explain, my mind still reeling from all the things. Iris and Dean know each other? She's marrying his nephew? Two presumed dead relatives now alive, and my mom is the villain? I can't even with any of this. So I focus on what I can in hopes that it will be enough.

"The last piece is in a secret tomb hidden underneath ancient ruins," I explain.

"Any idea where this tomb is?" Dean asks.

My face falls. "I don't know. I'd recognize it if I saw it again. It's very distinctive, and is next to a large fountain that still flows with water. I don't think it's on this world, though."

"How do you know that?" the man they call Sly asks.

"The ruins and the fountain were made of dragon bones, and dragons flew in the sky above," I say, still marveled by the vision of the mythical beasts taking flight.

"Nirandel," the three of them say together.

"We'll have to go there," Iris says.

Sly frowns. "That's not a stable place to be right now. The political conflicts between the Ashwraiths and Queen Sky's kingdom are still tense. There are rumors of an illegal slave trade between earth and Nirandel, and Queen Ilian of the Ashwraiths doesn't appear very interested in doing anything about it. You would be at grave risk traveling there."

Dean paces the room, frowning. "We have to risk it," he says. "If Levi saw what was in Alex's vision, he'll know what it means. He's probably already on his way there right now."

"Then there's no time to lose," I say. "But… any chance I can borrow of change of clothes, Iris?" I look down at Dean's too baggy pants and shirt and feel confident they'd be a liability if we have to fight or move quickly.

Iris nods. "Gotcha covered. Anything else?"

"Anyone have a spare ice ax or two?"

Iris laughs and grabs my arm. "I'll see what I can do." She looks to Sly and Dean. "We'll be back. Uncle, could you get word to Elias that I might be indisposed for a few days?"

Sly nods, frowning thoughtfully. "You sure you don't want me to send for him? He'd be a powerful ally in this fight."

Iris sighs. "I know, but he's got his hands full with a realm to run. I don't want to distract him. We got this. With Theo all powered up as the Storm Spirit, I think we can handle what Levi throws at us."

As we leave, I press into Iris. "Spill the beans. You've been holding out on me."

She chuckles. "Too many of my secrets aren't mine alone to share. It's not that I didn't trust you."

"I can certainly relate to that," I say.

"Here's the Reader's Digest version. There a Council of Hunters tasked to oversee the paranormal world on earth. I'm a Watcher, which is a big deal. Elias, my fiancé, used to be my mark. Number One on the Most Wanted list. He was very proud of that," she says with an affectionate chuckle. "At any rate, we defeated a big baddie that turned out to be his sister, and my kitten—who's always been a manticore—is now the Storm Spirit of Avakiri, the Fae world on Inferna. So he's super powerful. I'm still a badass. My fiancé is still a hottie. We rescued his mother, who's Queen of Inferna and Midnight Star of Avakiri, but his dad, the king, is still missing. We're working on that. And my Uncle Sly, who raised me, runs The Black Lotus, which is where we are right now and is a paranormal safe space and hotel for all manner of creatures from the nine worlds."

She says this last part as we walk through the main hall and I marvel at everything around me. Creatures I don't recognize walk by us, nodding to Iris before going about their business. A large tank takes up one wall but is empty save for water. "What's in there? A sea monster?"

Iris grins. "No, usually Marasphyr, the mermaid. But she's preoccupied these days pretending to be queen of the merepeople in Avakiri. It's a long story."

"You've had… quite a life," I say, stunned. I thought I knew so much, but even my own world is bigger and full of more mysteries than I could have ever imagined. Not to mention eight other worlds!

"Indeed I have." We exit the Black Lotus and enter a field of flowers with a few llamas gently grazing. "Those are my babies," she says, pointing to them. "I'll introduce you once we're out of this crisis."

She takes me to a beautiful manor and into her bedroom, but turns to me first. "The woman at your house?"

I can tell she knows the truth, but is waiting for me to say it. "It was my mother. She didn't die as I had thought. She was turned."

Iris nods. "I'm really sorry. I recognized her from the pictures around your place. She's working with Levi?"

"It appears so."

Iris just shakes her head. "Families are complicated." Then she turns and rummages through a trunk of clothes, tossing me things as she finds them. I change quickly into leather pants and a leather halter. It's a bit confining, and not my normal style, but I feel pretty badass.

"The leather helps," she says. "It's not just to look cool. It acts as lightweight armor and is spelled to be even more protective than normal leather."

There are straps on the side of each leg for holding weapons, and she digs through another trunk full and pulls out two pick axes, handing them to me. I test their weight and sharpness and marvel at the intricate design on the handles. "These are gorgeous!"

She shrugs. "A gift from the Dwarves of the Mead-owglades for saving them from a renegade giant. Not my style though. You can have them."

There's a whole story there, and I imagine a million other stories to be shared between the two of us. "When this is done, we need to get liquored up and spend a night catching up," I say.

She grins. "Deal. I have just the thing." The glint in her eyes makes me worry for the aftermath of that night, but hell, if I survive this, I'm okay with a little hangover.

"So," she says as we head back to Sly's office. "Tell me what's up with you and the Prince of Lust. I've never seen him so besotted before."

I sigh. "It's complicated."

Iris just laughs. "It's always complicated with the Vane men, I think. Just roll with it. He's a good man. Elias speaks highly of him, and you two… we'll, you're a perfect match aren't you?"

She's not wrong, which is why this is so hard. Falling for the kind that killed my father and turned my mother. Falling for a prince from another world. Falling for a man who will live forever, while I will age and die unless I want to be turned too.

Like I said. Complicated.

When we return, Dean raises an eyebrow and low whistles. "You should stock more of these outfits in your wardrobe, Dr. Stone. It suits you."

I grin. "Maybe I will. You know, if we survive this."

Iris rolls her eyes and her kitten meows with tiny ferocity. "You really need to have a better outlook. Don't manifest negativity. Believe in yourself."

I laugh. "I see you've been reading those self-help books I gave you."

"You should take a refresher course," she says. "There's some good shit in them."

Sly claps his hands together. "If you're going to Nirandel, be ready for anything. The dragons on Queen Sky's side should be safe enough, for dragons. But the Ashwraith's have been harvesting their own eggs and raising dragons as weapons of war. Be careful. You don't want to cross them."

"Super," Iris says. "Sounds fun. Shall we go?"

Sly nods and takes us through the hall and out a side entrance that leads to a spacious covered stone patio dotted with wild flowers, lush trees and featuring a large fountain in the center.

"I trust one of you has a location in mind?"

He looks to Dean first, but Dean shrugs. "I haven't been to Nirandel in ages."

Iris sighs. "It would be so much easier if we could travel there by mirror."

I raise an eyebrow and turn to my friend. "How can you travel by mirror?" I ask. "I thought only vampires could do that?"

Iris shrugs. "Another long story. Short of it is, I'm technically a vampire. One of the original vampires, actually. The Unseen Lord. Super badass. I just don't need blood like the lesser vampires do."

Dean huffs at that. "I'm older than you, remember that."

She laughs. "That might be sort of true, but not technically. Technically, I'm your great great great aunt or something. To be honest, I'm not sure how many greats there are since I was living in a tree for most of that time."

This conversation is so confusing. "Wouldn't that make you related to your fiancé?" I ask.

"That's a whole other story," Iris says. "Short version, no. Elias's father was turned, not born, into the Vane family. I'm technically Dean's dad's sister. I'll have to draw a family tree someday to show you. It's complicated."

"No shit," I say, my head spinning. "I'm really going to need more information about, like, everything, when all this is said and done." I shake my head, bemused by it all. "So if we can't travel by mirror, how do we get there?"

Sly leads us to the fountain and pulls out what looks like a few coins with ancient glyphs on them. "One to get there, one to get back. Don't lose it." He hands them to me.

"Um, why am I getting these?" I ask.

"You said there was a fountain as part of the ruins. You saw it, which means you are the only one who can hold the location in your mind and take everyone else there."

I stick one of the coins into my pocket and hold the other in my hand. "So, I just imagine it and… what? Jump in?"

Sly nods.

"Alrighty. Let's do this." Dean, Iris and I step up to the edge of the fountain, and I fold my fingers over the coin and picture my vision in my mind with as much detail as I can. Something tells me getting lost in a fountain portal wouldn't be the best way to end my day.

With a little nerves and a lot of faith I jump into the water. Dean follows, with Iris right behind him, but as the water opens into a vortex of light to suck us in, an explosion shakes the foundation of the fountain, and Iris falls back with a cry as a burst of magic pierces her chest, cutting a hole straight through where her heart should be. I scream and try to claw my way back to the surface, but we are too far gone. The portal doesn't give us up, and as we slide into another world, I see the half maimed face of Levi leering at me.

ALEX STONE

*T*he moment we arise from the fountain into the world of Nirandel, Dean grabs me and pushes me behind him as he pulls out his sword. As disoriented as I am, I follow suit and grab both of my axes, ready to face whatever I must, though I know in my gut our weapons are futile against Levi with the power of three Star shards.

Dean's brother stands opposite us, his skin glowing with magic, my mother by his side, eyes wide, fear on her face.

I push down the grief at seeing Iris killed. There's no way she could have survived that. But I can't mourn her right now. I have to stop this asshole first.

Levi is practically floating with the power of the Star shards. I can feel the magic pulsing, crawling over my skin and through my veins. Waves of nausea roll through my stomach as bile forms in my throat. This corruption of the Star's power is making me physically ill.

"I knew I could count on you to lead us to the Star, Dr. Stone," Levi says with a sneer. "Your help will no longer be needed."

With the dark power building in him, he reaches his arm out, extending it towards me. Dean tries to block the now black, smoke-like magic tearing across the fountain, and it hits him in the shoulder, slicing through skin and bone as it makes its way to me. My mother screams. "Don't! Don't hurt her. We might still need her to navigate the tomb. The Star won't be in an obvious place," she says.

Dean falls to his knees, his face pained, but he doesn't scream, even as blood pours from his wound. The smoke pauses just before it reaches me, and I can feel it seeking me out, curious.

Levi considers my mother's words and lowers his arm. "Why do we need her?" he asks. "You're an archeologist. You can find the Star for me."

She steels herself against his gaze. "Do you think I will help you if you kill my daughter?"

"Let him," I say. "Let him kill me. I will never help him."

I spit in Levi's direction, my axes at the ready, though completely useless.

He just laughs. "Like mother, like daughter." He points his hands towards Dean again, and the dark smoke coils around him. Dean screams, choking on the toxic magic, his body contorting in pain.

"Stop it!" I scream, thinking quickly. I can't give him the shard, not even to save Dean's life, but there has to be another way. "I'll help you. Just don't hurt him."

Levi drops Dean's body, and I rush over to him, helping him up. He's shaking, but he's strong. He leans into me, whispering in my ear. "I hope you have a plan."

"I'm working on it."

He looks worried, but what other choice do I have? I need to buy us some time.

Gripping his hand, I pull him forward as he rips off his

shirt to use it as a bandage against his arm. Even through the pain he winks at me.

"See? Wearing a shirt can come in handy," I tell him.

"Nah. If I didn't have one, I'd just borrow yours. Bigger win for both of us."

I roll my eyes, but then remember what we just left, and my heart sinks. "Iris. He killed Iris."

Dean shakes his head. "She's the Unseen Lord. She's not easy to kill. She'll regenerate, but she won't be able to get here. We're on our own."

"I... I don't really know how to react to that right now."

"Hurry it along, people. Power awaits," Levi says, stroking the shards at his waist.

Right. I have to help the bad guy. "Give me a second to get my bearings," I say, taking a moment to look around.

We arrived just where I intended, and everything matches my vision. I look up, and in the pale blue sky I see wings stretching wide, casting a long shadow over the hills in the distance. I suck in my breath as the dragon soars overhead, majestic with scales of blue jewel tones that flash against the light of the sun.

When I lay my hand on the fountain, made from the remains of dragons, I feel the energy in this world, how it was shaped by the dragon's breath, how it took form out of the bones of the dragons. When I open my eyes, the Star shards glow brightly on Levi's hip, and the world looks different. A magical trail of white light leads me forward, and I follow it as if in a trance.

Dean doesn't let go of me as we walk towards the ruin. An ancient stone stairway descends into an underground entrance covered with hanging vines that have climbed and crawled over and through the stone engravings and pillars framing the door.

Using one of my axes, I chop away at the aggressive

foliage. Dean helps with his sword, but Levi and my mother just watch and wait. I feel her fear and his impatience and anger. Both exhaust me as I struggle to figure out how to stop Levi before it's too late.

I can already feel the toll the use of the Star's power is taking. It is robbing the life of hundreds of people each time Levi uses it. Stealing pieces of them. Leaving them weaker to fuel the power needed. And it's giving Levi more life. He's become stronger, more dangerous, with each new shard found, and with each use of its power. I'm running out of time.

Once the door is cleared, Levi shoves me out of the way to study it. Then he uses the shards to blast it with power, hoping to break it down.

Nothing happens.

"Get this open," he shouts, his anger overcoming him.

I lay my hand on the stone and close my eyes. It speaks to me, but its voice is muted. Muddled. The door has seven concentric rings carved into it, each with different symbols, though they are covered with so many layers of sediment they're hard to decipher. "We have to position these symbols in the right order," I tell them. "That will unlock it."

"Then do it," Levi growls. "That's why you're still alive, after all."

Right. The circles move with great reluctance, slowed by age and time, the stone grinds together as if waking from a long winter slumber.

I try a few configurations to no avail. Dean runs a hand over one, and pauses, then asks to borrow my axe.

I hand it to him, and he uses it as a chisel to reveal more of the symbol on one of the rings until it's decipherable. He then holds up his arm, revealing the demon mark on his wrist and compares the two. "What do you think?" he asks.

I peer closer. "It's incredibly stylized, but yes, it could be a match."

His eyes light up. "Help me clear away the others."

We work silently, using my axes with care as we chip away at the wall, until all seven symbols are more easily read. Dean sucks in a breath as he studies it. "The rings are the Seven Realms of Inferna," he says softly. "But... that makes no sense. Why would they be here, in Nirandel?"

"I don't know, but if that's true, then we need to align the symbols to the correct realm," I say.

He nods and begins working. I don't know the demon symbols of each of his brothers, but he does. Levi looks on with interest, but says nothing and offers no help.

The largest circle is the hardest to move, and it takes both of us all our effort to budge it from its spot. Once we set it in place with King Fenris's demon mark visible, we step back and wait.

Nothing happens.

At least not at first.

Then, the ground beneath our feet shake, and within the wall stone and metal groan and grind together, moving for the first time in who knows how long.

A thrill travels up my spine. Despite the stakes, despite the circumstances, this is my calling. This is where I feel most alive. When I step into the timeless places where the past has gone to die and explore what still remains. Unearthing history makes me feel alive. So when the door splits in half and pulls itself open, revealing a dark hall covered in so many spider webs it will be impossible to walk through without hacking them away, I don't hesitate to step in.

And Dean is right by my side. I can tell by his face he's having the same experience as me. We are both seekers of the lost, of the ancient, of the historic. We share that bond. That thrill.

I grab a torch from the wall and Dean lights it. We move slowly, our boots crunching spiders moving underneath the white, haunting layers of webs that surround us on all sides. From a distance it might look like snow, but up close you can see it move, writhing from the many bugs trapped, the many bodies moving around their prey.

With my axe I hack away the webs that block our passage forward, ignoring Levi and my mother who follow, keeping my attention on my work and on Dean. Of the four of us, three of us are archeologists and know more or less what we're doing. That thought gives me some comfort.

I always wanted to go on a dig with my mother, but this isn't how I imagined it.

The reality would break my heart if I let it, so I shove that aside for now and keep my eyes forward. It's all I can do.

I feel the last shard calling me, pulling me to it. It lights a fire in my gut, my heart racing faster, the closer we get.

A thick layer of webs blocks our way, and Dean uses his sword to tear open a section for us to walk through. His body is slick with sweat, and I can tell his shoulder wound still pains him, but he keeps at the work.

When we step through the webs, I suck in my breath, and Dean pauses beside me.

"What's the holdup? Keep moving," Levi shouts, but even he falls silent when he sees what we see.

The hall we took to get here has opened up to a cavern filled with the tiny corpses of children. Dean and I walk through, studying them. They've been buried with stones in their mouths and lead on their eyes. Their bodies are wrapped in cloth. There are hundreds of them, maybe thousands, tunneling through the cavern. "What is this?" I ask. But I know. Because I've seen something similar on earth. "These children were all given vampire burials," I say. "Or a variation of that. I've seen this before. But it's not that common. On earth, vampire children were unearthed from the 5th century. They were buried with stones in their mouths to keep them from rising from the dead as vampires and spreading disease. The children mostly died of malaria, or other contagious diseases, and because little was known about the decomposition of bodies, superstition suggested vampires could eat their way out of the graves. Thus, the stone in the mouths. But... why would they be here? Now? Guarded by a door with Inferna Realms on it? And in such numbers?"

Dean's eyes widen and he hangs his head. "I know what this is." He turns to look at me, his eyes full of sorrow. "Superstition isn't just a human failing. Vampires have them too. These are the bodies of children born deformed, of still-births, or of children who developed deformities later in life and died in unusual circumstances. The superstition of our world was so strong that the bodies were taken to another world and buried here."

"What did vampires fear would happen if the remains weren't handled this way?" I ask, my inquisitive nature always at the ready for new information about a culture or history of a people.

Dean shrugs. "War, famine, disease, the usual fears."

Having seen and studied so many histories and ways of handling the transitions of birth and death, this news doesn't alarm or shock me. Rather, it's a new piece of information, and another realization that humans and vampires aren't as different as I once imagined. We are both a people filled with dark and light, flaws and redemptive qualities, bloody histories and hope for the future.

Levi finally finds his voice and shoves me forward. "Enough. This isn't what we're here for. Keep moving."

The cavern of dead children takes an unknowable

amount of time to cross. With my heightened powers I can see pieces of the lives lost here. "Not all of these children died naturally," I say, my throat constricting. "Many were killed, often violently, for being different."

Dean says nothing, only nods in a sad confirmation of my words.

Why must we all be so terrified of those who are different? It's a question I can answer from a sociological perspective, even a cultural anthropological perspective. But the answers, the knowledge about our natural and ingrained tendencies fall flat when faced with the reality those tendencies create.

We must rise above our base urges to murder and maim out of fear of displacement, out of the primal urge to conform or die as an outcast of our tribe. We cannot rise to the higher calling of our souls if we are forever stuck in the fear-based mindset of our egos.

With a sad sigh I move forward, out of the den of dead children and into another room, where the stone floor is covered in water growing with god knows what and filled with hundreds of different flowers that float atop. The water reaches my ankles, and I step carefully, unable to see to the bottom through the muck and flowers. Across from us is a bend in the stone wall that looks like it might be an opening, so I make my way there, but as Levi and my mother follow Dean and me, a trap is sprung.

I turn and pull out my axe, aiming it at the door we came through that's now grinding to a close. With precision, I throw the axe and it catches the bottom of the door, holding it open the width of the spike.

Dean raises an eyebrow. "Nice throw, Dr. Stone."

I can't help but grin in relief. "Thanks, it might be our only way out."

Just as the words leave my lips, the heavy stone door

crushes my axe, closing completely, and the room begins to fill with water, trapping us.

And once again I'm thrust back into the exciting game of how will Alex die today? Drowning, or at the hands of a psychopath vampire bent on destroying all the worlds?

ALEX STONE

"The room is a trap," my mother says, stating the obvious.

"So *untrap* it," Levi growls.

This man is seriously all charm. *Insert eye roll here.*

I'm not terribly worried about getting us out of here. I've been in worse jams than this, more or less. I mean, the being held hostage by a crazy vampire part is new, but otherwise, this is a fairly standard run-of-the-mill booby trap situation. I just have to find another door.

I continue onward, heading towards the part of the wall that looks promising, when my unflappable optimism takes another hit.

The walls screech, grown, and begin to close in.

And the ceiling is in on the action, lowering slowly onto us.

We will soon be squished like a marshmallow in a S'More if I don't get my ass in gear. I dash to the other side of the room and study the sliver of a crack in the wall. A small ridge extends out, like a saucer or a shallow bowl. A riddle is carved into it, but not in a language I recognize. I call Dean over. "Can you read this?" I ask him.

He nods. "It says, 'only the sly may enter'."

The water is rising, flowers sticking to my body as it reaches my chest. The walls and ceiling are closing in, and the four of us are pushed into the center with only an arm's length separating us from our bloody, broken ends.

I repeat the riddle in my head. There's something tickling the back of my mind, but it's so out of context I can't quite reach it. I close my eyes and focus, ignoring Levi's urges to hurry up, ignoring my mother's pleading eyes, grasping on to the confidence I see in Dean's face. He believes I can figure this out. I know I can. I must. Too much depends on it.

Only the sly… the sly… "Sly!" I scream, my eyes popping open. "Sly, from the Black Lotus. The door wants an offering. A flower. Quick, everyone, search the waters for a black lotus. Hurry!"

My words pump adrenaline into everyone, as the water threatens to overcome us in short order. We splash through the water, ducking beneath it, searching amongst hundreds of flowers that must be magically induced to stay in perpetual bloom. I toss aside a red rose, a blue carnation and a silver daffodil that's actually quite stunning, but definitely not the point.

"Found it!" Dean says, holding up the black flower in triumph.

The dark petals of the lotus brush against my skin like velvet as he hands it over to me and I study it. The water is now too high for me to stand. Dean, being taller, still has a few inches, but I'm forced to tread water to reach the door, while delicately cupping the lotus so as not to crush it. I place the flower on the small stone dish with the riddle inscribed, and I cross my fingers.

The flower glows darkly, submerged in the dirty water.

The smell is noxious—like rot and mildew, and it permeates my skin, though the leather outfit Iris provided seems to be doing a good job of keeping that portion of my body protected. I might just have to upgrade my wardrobe, assuming I survive this.

The walls push into us, forcing Dean and me into Levi and my mother. We are completely submerged now, without any room to come up for air. The pressure builds, pain flaring as bones and joints are bent against the unyielding stone. Levi attempts to use the shards to shatter the walls, to no avail.

And then, as suddenly as it began, it stops. The walls halt. The water begins to drain. And the crack where I placed the flower groans to an open, with just enough room for us each to squeeze through.

We step into the next cavern looking like drowned rats. Levi is furious, but silent as he wordlessly propels us forward into a space that is once again filled with dead children, this time covered in spider webs like the ones we fought through in the first hall. These remains are different, however. There are no stones in the mouths, no iron on their eyes. They are not wrapped in cloth. And their bodies haven't decomposed at the rate one would expect. They look relatively fresh. And there are no infants. All these children are at least ten to twelve years old, and all perfectly formed. Except that their eyes and mouths have been sewn shut. I shudder at the sight of it. This isn't something I've ever seen before.

"What is this?" I ask into the silence.

Dean stands beside me, studying them. "I have no idea."

"It doesn't matter," Levi says, shoving into us. "Find the shard."

In the center, a huge web is wrapped around something that is waist high. I walk carefully towards it, my axe out, studying the shape. "Help me," I tell Dean, as I delicately cut through the sticky white tendrils.

As we pierce through layers, a white glow pulses through what remains. In the end, we reveal a pedestal with the final shard resting on it.

I step back, sweat mixing with the vile water coating my skin, my eyes burning.

"There you go, Levi. It's all yours."

Dean looks ready to object, but I caution him with a glance and he stays silent.

Levi just laughs. "Do you think me a fool? It's likely trapped. You fetch it and bring it to me," he says from the spot we first entered through.

Eh. It was worth a try.

I use my gifts to see into the space, to identify the connections and networks, to read the room, as it were.

This one can't be claimed with a simple trick, like replacing it with a bag of rice. But I'm not seeing another way around this. I know it's trapped, I just don't know how.

I approach it cautiously, holding my hand out to touch the shard.

As I make contact, a vision overtakes me. One that upends my entire world, my entire existence. One that finally locks into place the last pieces of understanding. Tears fill my eyes as I lift the shard, almost against my will, my hand acting of its own accord. When the vision fades, I am faced with a new and shattering truth.

I open my eyes and find everyone staring at me. I look down and realize I am glowing. Levi, in fury, races towards me and grabs the shard from my hands. As he does, the tomb comes alive. All the dead children rise in unison, pushing past spider webs, their eyes and mouths still sewn closed. They move towards us and begin emitting a strange, dark sound, guttural and evil. And then tiny spiders emerge from their mouths, their ears, their eyes, crawling over their faces as they approach us.

Dean raises his sword and slashes at one of the dead children, severing it in two, but more keep coming, swarming him as they leap through the air like small, violent, acrobats, latching on to their victim. The vampire goes into rage mode, tearing them apart one by one as they clutch him, small hands winding around his throat in a desperate attempt to choke out his life.

Another child comes for me, but my mother screams and runs forward, pushing me aside and attacking the creature. The child corpse falls on her, and they roll to the ground. Another two pounce her, pinning her to the ground as spiders find purchase on my mother's skin, digging into her as she screams and fights. One child chokes her while the spiders continue eating away at her flesh. I need to stop this!

Frantically, I tear the shard from Levi's grip and place it back on the altar. The children freeze, their hands falling away from Dean and my mother, and they collapse to the ground as the spiders crawl back into their dead bodies.

All is instantly calm.

Dean runs over to me, clutching my arm. "Are you okay?"

I nod, but notice my mother is still on the ground, unmoving, her body shuddering with wounds that look poisonous. She's still breathing, but barely.

"We can't remove the shard from the pillar," I say, my voice hoarse. "The pieces have to be put together on the pillar. Give them to me!"

Levi, predictably, shoves me out of the way and into Dean's arms, as he stalks to the remaining shard. "You think I'm going to let you have the power for yourself. Stupid girl." His eyes glow with malice as he unlatches the pieces from his belt and clicks them into place. As each piece is returned, it fuses with the others, until all four are together at last.

The Fallen Star of Nirandel is beautiful. Breathtaking. It's an egg shaped orb that glows with so much power it's nearly blinding, and it calls to me. Sings to me in an ancient song that fills my soul with something new and unexpected.

Levi smiles, jubilant at his success. "Finally I shall be restored to my proper power. I will take over Inferna, claim my rightful place, and use the blood of the Unseen Lord to wipe away the sun and give vampires the rule of all the worlds at last!"

Just add a throaty "mwahahah" at the end of that and you have a proper cartoon villain speech, I swear to god. This guy is ridiculous.

Levi lifts the Star off the pedestal, and Dean braces for battle, but the zombie children do not come back to life. I knew they wouldn't.

Just like I know what's going to happen next.

But why spoil the surprise?

Levi does what any villain would do who has been granted all the superpowers he ever wanted. He channels that power and proceeds to kill us all.

Bad guys win.

The End.

Ha! Just kidding! I wouldn't leave you hanging like that.

But he does try to kill us all. He sucks in the power and points it at us. Dean looks at me and, noticing how chill I am, relaxes. I realize his trust in me runs deep. This makes me a bit glowey inside, but I still have a bad guy to defeat and my mom to check on, so I'm going to have to wait on exploring those feelings.

"Any last words before I disintegrate you all?" Levi asks.

And I'm actually touched he's giving us this. It's considerate, for a supervillain.

"Nah, I'm good." I turn to Dean. "You?"

Dean shakes his head. "I think we're okay here. Fire away, brother. Do what you've always wanted to do."

Levi cocks his head at that, a little confused, but so confident in his next move he doesn't pause to consider it.

His bad.

Because when he tries to use the power of the Star, his face turns ashen, his body shakes and spasms, and he falls to the ground, growing weaker rather than stronger. "What did you do?" he asks as the Star falls out of his hand and rolls over to me.

I pick it up and stroke it, feeling the warmth of the power flow into me. "Oops, my bad. There was one little detail I forgot to tell you. This," I say, holding up the egg, "was never the Fallen Star. It's a price of the power. It drains life, but it can't give it. You wanted to power up, but you actually just sucked your own life-force right out."

"What are you talking about?" he asks, his voice weak, his breath shallow. "If that's not the Star, what is?"

I see the moment realization dawns on Dean's face. He's a smart boy, that one.

"I've been the Fallen Star of Nirandel all along, asshole. And next time you see me, you'll be in chains."

ALEX STONE

I know. Massive plot twist for everyone. Myself included.

My bravado fades as Levi passes out. "Secure him," I shout to Dean before running over to my mother, the egg I was born in still clutched in my hand.

I drop to my knees and cradle her in my arms, tears flowing freely down my face. "Mom. Are you okay?"

The night she died flashes through my mind, the blood, the agony of my heart breaking. It's all happening again.

I can't bear it. Can't bear to lose her again. Not like this. Not when she risked her life to save mine.

I don't care that she has done awful things. I know her. I know who she is. I know she was just trying to protect me.

Her eyes open, but they are stained with red lines, and blood trickles out of them instead of tears. "My darling. You finally know the truth," she says in gasps.

"How? How did I end up with you and dad? Why did you never tell me?"

She takes my hand and places it on her forehead, and with a start I fall into a memory.

My mother, looking younger than I remember her, is on a dig. My father is with her, which isn't the norm, but he did sometimes join her for a time between movies. They look like a movie star couple on set, playing the part of archeologists rather than actually doing the work of them. My mother is exploring a crater created by something the locals said fell from the sky the night before.

Early reports called it a meteor shower that unearthed ancient remains, which intrigued the university my mother worked for, and so they sent her to investigate.

But she found something she never expected deep within the caves created by the shower. A shard of something full of power. Of magic she didn't believe in. Her scientific mind struggled to align itself with this new reality. My father, ever more open-minded and whimsical, embraced the idea of it being something from another world. My mother didn't believe it until she heard a noise. Digging through dirt, they found the source.

A baby.

Me.

Glowing white, like a star fallen from the sky. Like the shard in her hand.

They couldn't explain the existence of a magical baby any more than they could explain the magic in the shard, and so my father smuggled me and the piece out of the dig site, and my mother stayed to create a cover story and give instructions for the team to continue without her.

My mother faked a pregnancy and welcomed me into the world officially several months later. My father had connections and was able to get me fake papers to solidify my identity as their daughter. They hid the shard, raised me, and never told a soul the truth. The other pieces were assumed to have split during the descent, scattered across the world.

Through this connection I can feel the love my mother

felt for me, and still feels. I was always hers and my father's. No question.

Levi was the one who figured out she had the shard, but never suspected the truth about me. And so, to protect me and my secret, she did his bidding and became his slave. He abused her, and stalked me to show how susceptible I was to his wrath. She had no choice. At least, she didn't believe so.

I pull my hand away from her head and lean into her, holding her close to me. "I wish you'd told me. I wish you'd come to me. I could have helped you."

"I wanted you to live your life, my love. I thought, maybe I could even bring your father back. Make us a family again."

I look at the egg glowing next to me. Dark thoughts fill my mind. The life I lived in the Mirror of Idis. "I still could," I whisper, hating myself for what I'm saying. "With this, I could save you and bring dad back. But..."

I shake my head, and she slowly reaches her arm up and places her hand on my face. "But it would require you to steal from the lives of others. And you cannot do that. That's not who you are. Not who we raised you to be."

Her eyes flicker, and I know the spider venom is killing her too quickly. "Can you drink my blood? Dean's blood? He saved me from near death. Maybe he can save you."

She shakes her head, her eyes struggling to stay open. "I have done too much I regret in this life. You are my one redemption. It's my time. It was my time all those years ago when your father died. I should have died then. Let me be with him now. He's waiting for me. I can almost see him. Just behind the light. His hand is reaching for me. I'm coming, my love. I'm almost there."

And with those final words, her eyes close and her last breath leaves her. My heart breaks as I watch my mother die for a second—and last—time.

ALEX STONE

I'm frozen in time, paused in this moment of life and death, of choices that can make or break us.

My eyes seek Dean's, and he comes to me, wrapping his arms around me as I sob into his shoulders. We stay there longer than we should, as I mourn.

I hold the egg, stroking it, feeling the connection to my power. Light pours of it, surrounding my mother's body. At first I fear I am using the power to revive her, killing the innocent to quench my grief, but then I realize that's not the case.

From ashes to ashes. From dust to dust. The magic is taking back what my mother and Levi stole from it, and in the process, my mother's body is turned to dust, dissolving into nothing even as I clutch at what remains.

All I am left holding is the egg, now satisfied that its debt has been repaid. "This isn't safe, not in this world or my own. Not even with me. You don't know how close I came to using this power to save her."

He strokes my head. "You wouldn't have. I know you. I know your heart. You would always make the right choice."

"If she had begged. If she had pleaded for her life? I don't know."

He tilts my chin up to look him in the eyes. "I do. I know. I know you, Alex Stone."

"Still," I say, sighing. "We have to destroy it. And I finally know how."

He raises an eyebrow at that. "How then?"

"Let's get out of here and I'll tell you."

It's messy work, but I find us a shortcut and we exit the cave and make our way back to the fountain. Dean effortlessly carries Levi, taking great pleasure in 'accidentally' knocking his head against every hard surface he can.

Night has fallen in Nirandel, and three moons at different phases shine in the sky, illuminating a trio of dragons in silhouette. We're a few paces from the fountain, when the water splashes, and a burst of light shines out of it.

Dean drops Levi and pulls out his sword. I stand at the ready with my axe.

We both drop our guard in relief when Iris emerges, daggers drawn, kitten on her shoulder, ready to rumble. She looks disappointed to realize there's no one left to fight. "So you managed without me, then?" she asks, sheathing her weapons.

I tuck my axe back into my pants and rush over to hug my friend. "You really can come back from the dead!"

She laughs. "Oh yeah, I knew I was forgetting to tell you something!"

"Well, I have a few things to tell you too," I confess. "Get ready for a night of heavy drinking."

"I'm ready when you are."

She looks at Dean and takes in the scene before her. "So bad guy caught, but mom didn't make it?"

I nod, my eyes leaking again.

"I'm so sorry," she says. "That's truly awful."

Then she walks over to Levi's unconscious form and proceeds the vampire—hard—in the balls. Ouch.

That's going to hurt when he wakes up, and I don't care one bit.

"He'll have a new home in the dungeons of the Black Lotus," Iris says smugly.

"Is it secure?" I ask. I would hate to have to catch this asshole all over again.

Iris nods. "The most secure in the Nine Worlds. No one has ever escaped."

Dean clears his throat, and Iris laughs. "Well, okay, that's not entirely true anymore, but my escape was orchestrated, and Elias escaped because he planned to get caught."

"Wait, you and Elias were prisoners in the Black Lotus? And escaped?"

"Yeah, remember a while back when I went MIA and told you I'd had a spa vacation with no internet?"

"Yes…" I say, recalling how worried I was when I couldn't reach her.

"Well, I exaggerated the spa part a bit. But the no internet was true enough."

"My lord, woman," I say, exasperated.

Overhead the sound of flapping distracts us as a giant dragon descends from the above and lands near the fountain before us. Upon the dragon are a man and woman, both wearing crowns and dressed in silver and red.

"Oh, I should have said, I called for backup," Iris says, smiling, as the two slide off the magnificent beast and walk towards us.

"You might want to curtsy," Iris whispers, doing her best to take her own advice.

I mimic her movements and see Dean bowing deeply. "Your Majesties, it's an honor to see you again after so long."

The woman smiles, her eyes as dark as her hair, her skin

pale. "Please, let us not stand on formalities. We received word our help was needed, that a Fallen Star of Nirandel was in danger. But I see the Star is safe."

She looks at me with a knowing gaze. "I am Queen Sky, ruler of these lands. This is my husband, King Kaden. And you are the Fallen Star of Nirandel."

"I am," I say. "My name is Alex."

She dips her head in acknowledgment. "It is an honor to meet a Star in person. They are so very rare in recent history. Now, Alex, how may we be of service?"

Dean steps forward. "We're sorry to have disturbed you, but it seems the crisis is over. We will be taking my brother back to the Black Lotus for his sentencing."

The queen nods. "I was once from your world," she says to me. "And I too was thrust into another world, into powers I didn't understand, into a life that was new. Know that you have allies in us. This is your world, more than it is mine, even."

"Thank you," I say. "But I do have one request." I hold up the egg. "This can only be destroyed by dragon fire. Would your dragon be willing to destroy it?"

She raises an eyebrow at that. "What you ask comes with a price. Do you understand?"

I nod. "I do. I'm willing to pay it."

"Whoa, wait a minute. What price?" Dean asks, stepping towards me.

"It's nothing. It's fine. This power can't exist. It's too dangerous. Too easily abused. This must be done."

"But you'll be fine, right?"

I share a glance with the queen, then return my gaze to him. "Yes, I'll be fine."

"Alex, what's the price?"

I touch his cheek and kiss him softly on the lips. "Nothing you yourself wouldn't pay if you had to."

With that, I step away from him.

The queen lays a hand on her dragon. "This is Umi. He has agreed to do this for you. But you must hold the egg yourself."

I nod. I knew that would be required. I saw this in my vision. Amongst so many other things. Things I'll never be able to unsee. Things I might have, could have, done with this power were it to remain in me.

Dean and Iris look nervous, but the queen is calm as she places me safely away from the others and her dragon gets into position.

I take one last look at the world around me, savoring the layers of meaning and connection I see with my gift. Then I close my eyes, clutching the egg, and wait.

Umi breathes in a deep breath and then releases his flames. They do not burn as I imagine, but rather feel white hot, like ice and fire mixed together. It tears into my skin, through muscle and bone, through my very soul, until I feel myself turning to dust, losing myself entirely.

Everything within me is released. I float away on the wind, become one with the particles of air, dance happily through space and time, until I hear Dean call out, his anguish real, his pain raw and angry. He calls me back to form, to body, to the corporeal world. I fall into myself hard, heavy, new pains coursing through my body.

The dragon's fire is spent.

The egg I once held is gone.

I am naked, undone and remade, shivering in the chill of the cool night air, and the world is different.

Flatter.

Denser.

It no longer speaks to me.

Dean runs forward, pulling me into his arms. "What was the cost?" he asks again.

"My power. The cost was all my power."

"*W*hat does that mean?" Dean asks, though I can tell he has an idea.

"I can no longer sense artifacts, or see into the world around me. I'm normal." But it feels worse than normal. It feels hollow. Empty. This has always been a part of me. It's shaped my world. My work. Given me an edge. I don't know who I am without it.

Dean seems to read my mind as emotions flit across my face. "Whatever you are, you are far from normal. You're extraordinary, and you don't need a magical connection to be a badass archaeologist or whatever you choose to do."

I can't find the words to respond, and then, I feel a burning on my arm, pulsing beneath my skin.

I suck in my breath, tears filling my eyes as I scratch at the spot.

"What's wrong?"

He looks to the queen. "What's happening to her?"

Queen Sky smiles gently. "She gave up her gift, but the dragons, through Umi, have given her another, to thank her for her self-sacrifice. And to honor the Fallen Star of Nirandel."

The burning dulls, and in its place, a dragon mark wraps around my forearm. "What does it mean?" I ask, feeling something alight within my core.

Dean helps me stand, and the queen offers me her silver cape to wrap around my shoulders. I accept it gratefully.

"You will discover over time what gift they have given you," she says. "But I do know that as a Star, you are immortal, and that has remained. Whatever else might grow within you, only time will tell."

With heartfelt goodbyes, the king and queen mount Umi and take off into the sky. I am shaken, exhausted, and stunned by all that has taken place. Dean studies my arm in wonder. "You were born for great things, Dr. Stone."

"Right now I'd settle for a long bath and an even longer sleep."

Iris takes Levi back to the Black Lotus with promises that he'll be kept under lock and key, and Dean and I follow.

When we arrive, I pull Dean aside. "There's something else I have to tell you. I had another vision while holding the egg." I take a deep breath. "Levi has a prisoner being held in a secret cave of his old kingdom. It's the king. Your brother, Fen. Levi's been feeding off of him to maintain his strength while he hunted for the Fallen Star."

"Do you know where this cave is?" Dean asks.

I nod, then sway on my feet, the room around me spinning.

Dean catches me and settles me onto the couch. "I think I can find it, if you can get us close enough."

Dean shakes his head. "No way. You're not going anywhere after what you've been through. Draw me a picture and tell me all the details you can. I'll find it myself. You'll stay here and rest."

Dean looks to Sly. "Will you take care of her? Get her a healer? Food? Whatever she needs?"

Sly nods. "You know I will, Prince."

Dean nods as Sly hands me parchment and charcoal.

I close my eyes, picturing the scene in my mind, and I draw.

When I open my eyes, I stare, flabbergasted. "Did... did I draw that?" I ask.

Because honestly, if you'd asked me to draw anything a few weeks ago, it would have looked like a glorified stick figure. But this, what I'm holding now? It's a masterpiece. It shows a castle in full detail, and the path that leads to the cave. Trees and landmarks with shading, texture and depth. I could frame this and sell it on eBay for quite a sum.

Dean whistles through his teeth and Sly studies the mark on my arm. "You've been dragon-touched," he says in awe.

I nod.

"Then this is only the beginning," he says, nodding to my drawing.

Dean takes the parchment, studying it. "I know where this is." He stands, then sits back down to face me. "Are you okay if I leave?"

I roll my eyes. "I didn't turn into a helpless female just because I lost my powers. Go. Save the king. Be a hero. I'll be here eating and drinking and catching up with Iris. She owes me some stories."

He kisses me, and need grows in us both, but that will have to wait too. Then he rolls the parchment, sticks it in his pocket and walks to Sly's mirror. With a final glance to me and a flirtatious wink, he leaves through the mirror.

I sigh once he's gone, leaning back against the couch. Sly pours something amber from a crystal decanter and hands me the glass. "This will take the edge off," he says, pouring himself one.

"Now, tell me all about you and the delicious Prince of Lust."

ALEX STONE

I duck out of that conversation as quickly as possible, citing my desperate need for a bath—since I still stink of that awful water—and actual clothing. Sly guides me to a private room and ushers me in. "Stay here as long as you like. Consider the Black Lotus home whenever you're in need of one."

Remembering that my Malibu mansion is actually in pieces, I thank him. But before he leaves, I call out. "Sly... you set up that tomb, didn't you?"

He gives a bow of his head. "That was a very long time ago. And a favor to a powerful king who needed to appease his people's fears." He smiles, the years showing in his eyes. "You're a remarkable person for figuring it out."

I lower my eyes to hide the grief that wells up. "It was my gift. Nothing more."

"Malarkey," he says. "I spelled that tomb myself with magic even older than yours. It was you, dear girl. Never doubt it."

As he leaves, I consider his words and realize that though the Star shard was calling to me, I didn't actually use my powers to decipher the riddle or figure out the traps. A swell of hope grows in me. Maybe my career as an archeologist isn't over just because my gifts have changed.

With renewed spirit, I bathe and change clothes, then go in search of Iris. I find her at her house, playing a new video game on her PlayStation.

"Ready for that drink?" I ask.

She grins and turns off her game. "Sure thing. Where did your man go?"

I explain about finding Fen and she shrieks. "That's amazeballs. Elias is going to be so happy. But he can wait. Tonight, it's you and me time."

She pulls out a dusty bottle of something green and scary looking and waggles an eyebrow. "Ready for a night you'll never remember, but will change your life forever?"

"Um… maybe?"

She laughs and pours us both drinks.

The liquor burns going down, then fills me with warmth. I pet Theo, who purrs under the attention, as Iris and I share all our secrets, all our adventures, all the things we've been keeping from each other for so many years, thinking we were the ones with the biggest secrets.

I'm a Fallen Star. She's the Unseen Lord.

I'm a famous archeologist. She's a badass Watcher.

But tonight we're just two women getting drunk, letting loose, and enjoying a moment of respite in a world that sometimes feels a bit mad.

And while I can't wait to see Dean again, and explore whatever it is we have, and she surely is looking forward to being with her fiancé again soon, we also appreciate the importance of female friendships, of bonds that are thicker than blood, of moments that bind strangers into family.

FENRIS VANE, KING OF INFERNA, AN EPILOGUE

*T*he ride north is long and hard, and yet there is nowhere I would rather be, but back here, in the rugged wilderness of Inferna. I breathe in the scents of pine and earth and snow of my homeland. The realm of War. It has been many weeks since I left to search for Arianna, since Levi captured me and held me prisoner. I have been gone too long. I miss my wife. I miss my children. Yes, even Aya. Perhaps especially Aya. Though Dean told me of what she has done. Of how she bewitched her mother and fought against her brother. He also told me of how she did the right thing at the end. I hope she is safe. I pray she is happy.

My wolf, Baron, travels to my right, with Dean at my left, his horse prone to nipping at mine when too close. He talks often and about things of little importance, but I am glad for his company. And I suppose, beyond being my brother, he is also one of my dearest friends. Him, Kayla, and Asher are all very dear to me. And yet, I realize I have spent little time with them in these past years, having been so focused on ruling. Perhaps now I will make more time for friends. For family. Perhaps I can even grow closer to Ace and Zeb. For I thought about them often when locked away, inches from death. I thought of how sad it was, that I could die now, and not have truly known them.

The Prince of Lust looks around at the forest that surrounds our path, his face filling with awe. "Fen, can you believe it's been 100 years since you and I rode through these forests together, searching for Arianna? I swear, it feels just like yesterday."

Memories. Some fond. Some less so, flood my mind. And I look out onto the horizon with a smile. "Yes. I suppose it does." Dean chuckles, and I study his joyous face, a face happier than I have seen in a long time. "I'm glad for you, brother," I say. "Glad you have finally found someone to love. And who loves you in return. Alex Stone seems to be an amazing person."

He blinks, a twinkle in his eye. "That she is, brother. That she is."

We come upon a peak, and in the distance, I see it. Stone-hill. Home.

And without a second thought, I spur my horse on, making haste, charging down the mountain through snow and wind, a big, uncontrollable smile on my face. Baron joins me, as excited to be home with family as I am. And as soon as I am through the gates, I see her standing there. Waiting. My wife. My Arianna. Dressed in a gown of pure white, her black hair drifting gently in the breeze. I leap off my steed with reckless abandon and rush into her warm embrace. I clutch her tightly against my chest. I bury my face in her hair. I take in her sweet scent and every detail of her beautiful face and her gorgeous eyes. She is even more stunning than I remember. And yet she is the same as she has always been.

Her dragon, Yami, leaps from her shoulders onto Baron's head, the two of them excited to be together again. But I am focused solely on my wife.

I take her head gently in my hands, and I press my lips to hers, and I am overcome with a love that I cannot even begin to describe.

"Welcome back," she says. "Welcome back, my love."

"There were times I feared," I whisper. "Times I feared I would never return to you. But all I had to do was remember your voice. To remember *Dum Spiro Spero*. To remember to hope. And so I did."

It takes a moment, for I am so absorbed by her, to look up, and when I do I see my son. I see Elias. He greets me with a smile and clasps his arms around my shoulders. How long has it been since I last saw him? Since he last went into exile accused of horrible crimes not his own? Before I can even remember, his words pull me from my thoughts.

"I missed you so, father. It's been too long since we last went hunting together."

"Yes. Too long, my son." I pull him closer and kiss him on the forehead as a large black wolf walking by his side notices Baron. The two wolves, who clearly know each other, sniff and nuzzle each other, and my son grunts and steps back, beaming as he gestures to a woman at his side.

"Father," he says, clearing his throat. "This is my fiancé. Iris."

The woman has short black hair and a smile that is playfully devious, and she holds out her hand to greet me.

"It's a pleasure to meet you, sir. I—"

I wrap her in a hug, cutting off her words. "And it's a pleasure to meet you as well, Iris. I do not know you yet, but if my son loves you, then I am certain you are a wonderful person, and I can't wait to get better acquainted."

I step back, turning to Arianna. "Any news of Aya?" I ask, hopeful.

She shakes her head somberly. Then Iris, seeming to

notice our exchange, closes her eyes, and speaks as the wind picks up around her. "I can sense her," she says. "Aya is safe."

I do not know how she has this ability, but her words bring joy to my heart. Elias winks at me. "We have much to discuss, father."

"Yes. Yes we do." I stand between my son and my wife, holding each of them close, and together we ascend up the mountain. To my castle. To my Stonehill.

To my home.

ASHER VANE, PRINCE OF PRIDE, AN EPILOGUE

*L*ovely. The ship is taking us to the island in good time, but I spend most of the journey lounging on a pillow that is far too comfortable and snacking on grapes that are far too sour. The door creaks, and the most beautiful of men enters my quarters. His skin is gold like honey and covers thick chords of muscle underneath. His head, completely devoid of hair and covered in serpentine tattoos, is perfectly proportionate. His face is kind, and strong, and mesmerizing.

Varis meets my eyes. "You're doing it again."

"Doing what?" I ask, tossing the hundredth grape into my mouth.

"Brooding. You've been locked in this cabin all day."

I puff out my chest. "I do not brood. And if I do, I do so in enough style as to not make it brooding, but rather contemplating. Now come sit with me, my love."

He chuckles, removing the heavy white cloak of feathers around his shoulders, and joins me on the sofa, stretching his arm out behind me. "What's bothering you?" he asks, gently, stroking my hair with a soft touch.

I don't speak right away. Instead, I take in his scent, the fresh aroma of silver trees and the slight hint of gryphons, things so much a part of his homeland in the air tribes. And I lean my head against his chest, and feel his strong pulsing heart against my ear, and I think, this is the only person who truly knows me. The only person I feel so comfortably safe around. And then I proceed to tell him of my worries.

"Recently, I have felt this new feeling. And I don't know what to make of it, so yes, I have been in here all day, thinking on the matter, and I still don't know what to think."

His chest vibrates as he speaks. A strong warm rubble. "And what is this new feeling?"

"I feel... old," I say.

He laughs, and I feel the heat rising in my cheeks. Of course. Why would I, a vampire who has lived for millennium, always youthful in body and mind, suddenly complain about being old? How silly of me... he must think me foolish.

But then my love surprises me, as he often does. "I understand," he says tenderly. "Once, we were the true leaders of our people. Thousands looked up to us. Relied on us. We bore that great responsibility, because we were the only ones who could bear it. But now, the vampires have a new prince in Elias. And slowly but surely, he is taking on more and more obligations. Iris stands by his side, assisting and leading in all sorts of manners. And soon their children, if they choose to have children—and I suspect they will—those children will too become leaders. Even I, the Air Druid of my people, have seen Kayla take up many of my duties. And now, Arias, the new water druid, takes on even more. A new generation has come, my love. A new generation that does so well what we once thought only we could do. And so yes, I understand why you feel old. Because for the first time in my life, I feel the same."

I look up at his kind and glorious face, and I smile and touch his cheek gently.

"Varis, you are, and always will be, my Karasi. Spirit of my heart."

Our lips meet. I feel his hot breath mix with my own. We stay together for a while, holding each other, enjoying each other's bodies. Quite sometime later, and yet altogether too soon, we are interrupted by a knock on the door. "We have arrived," hollers a crewman from outside the cabin.

Finally. Hopefully I can feel useful once more. And forget all about feeling old. Even if just for a moment. Though, I suspect the worry will return to me in time.

Varis and I get dressed and depart our lodgings, stepping into the sunlight and looking upon the island where the ancient Storm Spirit once slumbered. The place is in ruins. Dead trees still cover much of the forest. Burned and crumbled buildings still litter the village.

This will not do. This will not do at all. The island needs even more help than I anticipated. Not only to repair, but to grow. This measly village could be a paradise of wonder and splendor. Who better than the Prince of Pride to endow some style and panache onto this little corner of life? Yes, indeed. This project is all I could have hoped for and more.

I'm pulled from my thoughts when I see my very good friends coming up to greet us. Tavian and Kayla. Looking as marvelous as ever. Tavian with that luxurious copper hair and olive skin of his. Kayla with her purple and silver phoenix perched on her shoulder, blue ponytail waving carelessly in the wind. I'm so happy to see them, I almost fail to notice the dirt on their leather clothes, or the slight stench of mud upon them. Almost. I mean... I am still the Prince of Pride, after all.

We hug and exchange greetings, laughing and smiling just because we can. And then the four of us, Kayla, Tavian, Varis, and I, descend from the ship and head into the village, observing the work that still needs doing.

"We are grateful for your help," says Tavian, clasping my shoulder. "Your crew should double our workforce and can make good progress before the next winter. We have families in need of homes. Though of course, they are being provided for, the circumstances are not ideal."

I nod. "Indeed. We came as soon as we heard of your peril. If you don't mind, I have some other suggestions and ideas to discuss with you soon."

Kayla squints her eyes at me. "You're not intending to add a hotel, are you?"

I raise my arm to my chest, aghast. "A hotel? Dear no, Kayla. Why stop there? I intend to add an entire resort and recreational park to this little slice of heaven."

She rolls her eyes at me, but smiles all the same, and I know she will agree with me eventually. In the meantime, there are more hellos to make. "Where is that boy of yours, Arias?" I ask.

"Likely helping the men on the hill," says Tavian. "He feels personally responsible for much of the destruction that occurred here. And he does his best to make up for it every day, I think. I will take you to him tonight, if you wish. But right now, you must be weary from your journey. Come. The inn is still functional. We have wine and ale and juicy roasted duck for you."

I lick my lips, in deep need of something other than nearly rotting grapes and bread.

"That sounds lovely," I say, following Kayla into the tavern.

The four of us order everything on the menu, a delectable selection of crab and lobster and moon fish, and of course the duck, along with a variety of cheeses and sweet meats, roasted veggies and powdered pastries. Though we start drinking early, we don't stop until late into the night, exchanging stories of our many years together and apart. At one point, Tavian falls over with laughter, and as I mention my little "honeymoon incident" Varis turns as red as a cherry. By the end, Kayla outdrinks us all, ordering another round while we're quite ready to call it a night. It is good to see my friends so happy. And I realize I missed them far more than I had thought. And that perhaps it will be a quite long while until I leave this little island.

I look at each of us. A druid, a vampire, an ancient Fae, and a Shade. All of us equals, all of us comrades. And for a moment, I cannot believe that the goal I set out to achieve so many years ago, of peace between our races, has finally been accomplished.

And an overwhelming sense of pride and love consumes me.

As the new round is served, I step away for a moment, grabbing some fresh air on a pier overlooking the water. The stars are shining brightly tonight, and the waters are calm and splendid for a swim. Perhaps I will take one later with Varis. But right now, I notice a figure in the distance. Arias, dressed completely in loose, white clothing, leaning down on one knee by the waves, his golden hair spilling over his shoulders. He is talking and smiling and laughing, and I follow his gaze to a most lovely creature. A mermaid laying on the beach, propped up on her elbows, listening intently to his every word, her cheeks flushing red. Even from this distance, I can tell they are in love. Ah, yes. Young love. How fiercely it burns.

It makes me think of my own youthful days. Of passionate affairs and causal dalliances, of dangerous flirtations and broken hearts. And yet, for all the excitement of those days, I would never trade them for the comfort and love I share with Varis now.

He comes out from the tavern, my glorious druid of the air, my wild one, and wraps his arms around me. "I missed you," he whispers. "What have you been up to, my love?"

"Thinking," I say, taking a deep breath. "Thinking that I am truly old. And that might be perfectly fine. Yes. That is perfectly fine indeed."

He kisses me upon the head, and I take his hand in mine, and together we turn around and walk back into the tavern, to be amongst friends.

ALEX STONE, AN EPILOGUE

"*T*his feels serious," I say, applying a coat of red lipstick to match my dress.

Dean comes up behind me and slides his hands around my waist, pulling me against his chest. He drops his mouth to my neck and bare shoulders, leaving hot kisses in his wake. His lips are close to my earlobe, sending shivers up my spine. "It's not that serious."

I twist to face him, our mouths inches apart. "Meeting your whole family for the holidays? That's serious."

I don't have a family. Haven't had one for so long I've forgotten what it feels like. Dean has a huge family, and they're royalty. It's a bit much.

"My brother owes you his life and already adores you. Ari knows you saved Fen, so she's been dying to meet you. Asher and Varis are coming back from the island just for this, and they're bringing Kayla, Tavian and Arias, Elias's twin brother. Iris and Elias will be there. You've been wanting to meet him, right?"

I nod. "That's true. But you just listed a lot of names I'm likely to forget." My nerves don't usually get the better of me, but this time they have. After everything we went through in stopping Levi and my mother, after losing her again, and losing any chance of seeing my father one last time, after destroying the Star of Nirandel and finding out the truth about myself... I needed time. Dean invited me to stay in his Pleasure Palace. Even offered to rename it, which made me laugh. It was a tempting offer, what with my mansion totally destroyed and all. But I wasn't ready to relocate to an entirely new world.

Iris's Uncle Sly offered to let me stay at The Black Lotus for as long as I wanted. I took him up on the offer, and I did a lot of thinking and sleeping and soul searching. I also spent time with Dean, but in normal ways. We went to eat and took in some shows. We discovered a similar taste in movies and plays. I spent time with Iris, though never got to see her fiancé since he was busy being a prince and all. Seems there are a lot of those to go around—princes that is. I'm still a bit in awe that I've found mine.

I know his family has been wanting to meet me, and I've put them off for months. Until now.

Now it's the holidays, and I'm ready to figure out the next chapter of my life. Apparently that includes meeting Dean's whole royal family at High Castle for a Winter Solstice celebration.

I step back and spin, showing off my new dress, hand sewn by his tailors, to conform to Inferna dress code. "How do I look?"

His eyes fill with desire, and I push him away playfully. "You'll ruin my makeup," I warn.

"Later, I plan to ruin that dress too," he threatens, and a thrill runs through my body in anticipation.

He is definitely a lover I have not grown bored of. But no wonder, given he is the Prince of Lust. It's a title well-earned, but doesn't do him justice, to be honest. There's so much more to him than desire. I've fallen in love with his mind, his heart, his very soul.

And yes, I now believe vampires have souls. I've met too many good ones to think otherwise. I still have the memories of what happened to my parents, of course, and they still sting, but that wound is finally healing after all these years.

I guess I can thank my mother for that, despite everything. And Dean.

I hold his hand as we cross over to the mirror Sly gave me for my room in the Black Lotus. He places a hand on it, and we transport into High Castle, a lavish medieval style estate that includes touches of modern life. A strange mix, but one I appreciate, as they use magic to replicate plumbing and some modern comforts.

I clutch his hand as we make our way to the banquet hall, and when we enter, I suck in a breath, transfixed. A huge table carved from stone edges the large room, with the king and queen at the head and chairs placed around facing the center, where a fire burns in a hearth and a live orchestra performs a haunting song.

The king has a large white wolf at his feet and is wearing a crown and red velvet robes. He smiles when he sees us, waving. His wife, Queen Arianna, sits beside him with a small dragon perched on her shoulder, dressed in similar style to him, her dark hair gleaming under the candlelight. The table and walls are strewn with holly and candles, the bright red berries contrasting with the forest green leaves. Red and green satin bows hold it all together, and in the corner the largest Christmas tree I've ever seen is set up and decorated with crystal balls of silver, and white candles that seem magicked to not melt.

Dean's other brothers are sitting around the table, and other members of their households I've not yet met are milling about talking, laughing and partaking of the massive feast. Every kind of cooked meat, fruit pies, vegetable casseroles, loaves of freshly baked bread, and candied dishes adorn the space, as well as bottles of wine and, I presume, blood. I'll have to make sure Dean steers me toward the wine. I made the mistake once of grabbing a glass I thought was wine and turned out to be blood. Not a mistake I want to repeat. Like…. Ever.

Fen stands when we approach, hugging Dean first, then me. "I'm so glad you both could make it."

"Thank you for inviting me," I say, unsure if I should curtsy or what? I look to Dean for guidance but he's no help.

"Alex, this is my wife, Ari."

The queen smiles and her baby dragon chirps and then hops over to me, sniffing my hand. "Yami likes you," she says. "That's a good sign. And we owe you so much."

Ari is beautiful, and clearly happy to be reunited with her husband at last. Fen offers us the seats near him, and we join them. Dean fills a plate for me and offers me wine with a wink, as if he's reading my mind. Then he leans over and points out all his relatives, telling me their names and reminding me about stories he's told to help me put faces to all them.

When Iris and Elias arrive, I breathe a sigh of relief. She smiles and heads straight for us, taking a seat at my side and hugging me. "I knew you'd come."

She introduces me to Elias, who is just as handsome as she described, and he and Dean share a meaningful look.

The festivities continue, and I meet other uncles—Ace the inventor, Zeb, Prince of Gluttony, Asher and his Druid partner Varis, and important members of the family. Too many names to remember, too much family to track, but it occurs to me this could be my family someday. Dean and I have talked about it, about where our future might lay, and neither of us imagines being with anyone else, but we're in no rush. There's time. Especially if what Queen Sky said is true, that I won't age, nor will I need to be turned to enjoy an immortal life.

Iris and I have more in common than one would have thought, each with our mysterious genesis into this world.

As we feast, drink and enjoy the entertainment, I settle into this feeling of being surrounded by a new kind of family and friends.

At one point Elias stands and pulls something out of his pocket. A sprig of mistletoe. He holds it over Iris's head and prepares to kiss her when all hell breaks loose. Literally.

She jumps back, toppling her chair in the process and spilling wine everywhere, then pulls out one of her daggers from… I'm not even sure where, and proceeds to slash the poor green sprig apart.

Elias stands, dumbfounded, staring at his fiancé. "What the hell was that?" he asks, though he doesn't look mad, just amused.

Iris squints her face as the music falls silent. All eyes are on her.

She looks around and sighs. "Oh, alright. If you must know. This," she says, gesturing to the bits of mistletoe scattered on the rugs, "is my third fear."

Elias nearly doubles over laughing. "This? A bit of a plant? This is what the greatest Hunter that ever lived is scared of? Oh come now, you must tell us why. This is too rich."

"Yes," Ari says, having laughed so hard tears are streaming down her face. "Please, Iris. Share. This must be good."

Iris rolls her eyes, tugging her emerald green dress into place and tucking her dagger back into its secret spot, then sits back down. "Very well. As some of you know, I fear only three things. Spiders," she says, shivering. I knew this of course, after her reaction to my story about the spiders in the tomb. "Being buried alive," she continues, and this is news to me, but come on, who wouldn't be terrified by that?

"And mistletoe toe," she concludes, to a few hushed snickers from her audience. "The reason for my first two fears are fairly obvious and are associated with traumatic experiences. Well, so too is this. Allow me to set the stage. It was the winter of my thirteenth year. I was a socially awkward newly minted teen who was more interested in swordplay and ways to kill and maim than in boys. But my best friend was a gorgeous succubus who couldn't help but attract all manner of creature to her. Male or female, it didn't matter. Everyone loved Callie. That year, Uncle Sly hired a decorator to deck the Black Lotus in the most spectacular holiday trim, and that included copious amounts of mistletoe hanging from every bloody doorway. It was really overkill if you ask me."

Iris pauses to sip from her refreshed wine glass, then continues. "At any rate, I was not interested in partaking of the mistletoe kiss. But Callie collected her share and more that season, and seemed hell-bent and determined that I too experience the wonders of said kiss. Since I had no desire to attract a male for this experience, she decided to use her charms for evil, and attract one for me. It was the night of the Solstice, and the Lotus was packed with revelers getting drunk on expensive liquor and enjoying the entertainment my uncle provided. On that fated night, a boy about my age approached me, and seeing that I was not, in fact, standing under the mistletoe, but was rather studying the room for emergency exits in case shit hit the proverbial fan, he deliberately bumped into me, thus knocking me under the doorframe. Now that I was standing under the mistletoe, he then proceeded to jam his tongue so far down my throat I was convinced he was going for my tonsils. I froze, initially paralyzed by the experience, the shock of it all, as his drool ran down my lips and face, and bits of his undigested dinner made its way into my mouth."

This elicits a few groans from everyone listening, and Iris crinkles her face and takes another drink. The rest of the table does as well. I'm sensing a new drinking game coming on.

"It gets worse, my friends," Iris says, grimacing. "So much worse. Once my instincts kicked back in, I freaked the hell out and kneed the kid in the groin, then prepared to body slam him into the wall, only when he doubled over from pain, he also bit down. Hard. So hard in fact, that he bit the tip of my tongue clean off."

I wince at the image and take another drink. So does Iris. So does everyone. Elias isn't laughing anymore and looks rather nauseous at this story.

"So, there I am, my tongue gone, blood gushing out of my mouth, as this prick rolls around on the floor crying, my tongue still between his teeth, when Uncle Sly runs over and is about to eviscerate the boy, until Callie intervenes and explains what she did. I was sent to the healer and spent Christmas regrowing my tongue by drinking the most vile potion you can imagine four times a day for four weeks. Callie was grounded for the same duration, and no underage boys were allowed in the Black Lotus for a good six months."

"What happened to the boy?" Elias asks.

Iris shrugs. "Never saw him again. He was either banished or too traumatized to ever return."

Elias takes Iris's hand and squeezes it. "You've had shit luck with men my love. Lucky I came along when I did."

She laughs and swats at him, but I can see the love in her eyes. In fact, there is so much love in this room. Ari and Fen are talking quietly together, their faces pressed close, hands in each other's. Asher and Varis laugh at a joke I'm not privy to, they're affection for each other clear. Kayla and Tavian have stolen more than one kiss that I've seen so far.

It feels good to be surrounded by this energy, and I reach for Dean's hand, giving it a squeeze. His piercing blue eyes land on mine, melting me to the core. A flush of heat surges in me and thoughts of what we will do later burn in my mind.

I realize then I've had enough time to myself. "Hey," I say, scooting closer to him.

"Hey yourself," he says with a grin.

"Is that offer still open?" I ask.

"Which offer might that be?"

"To live with you."

His eyes widen, and as an answer he pulls me into a kiss that makes all other kisses pale in comparison.

It takes all my self-control not to grab his hand and retreat to somewhere more private to see where else that kiss might go. "Is that a yes?" I ask, my lips still touching his.

"That's a yes."

I lean into him, and he holds me as we watch acrobats perform where the orchestra had been, enjoying the rest of the evening with our friends and family.

Later that night, while the candles burn low, we all crowd around the Christmas tree and exchange gifts. As we do, Iris comes to sit with us. "So, what does the future hold for you two lovebirds?"

I glance at Dean and shrug. "I'm not sure. But I'll be spending more time in Inferna, it appears. Since it looks like I'm moving here."

"And I've got a lead on a new dig site in Egypt," Dean says. "Where Akhenaten's staff might be. It's said to contain the power of the sun god, Aten, and has been attributed with powerful magic. What do you think? Want to partner up and find some hidden treasure?"

I smile. "Only if you'll reconsider your stance on museums."

He rolls his eyes. "We'll talk about it."

Indeed we will, I think, as the gift giving continues. I don't know what our future will hold, but I feel certain we'll face it together. Whatever it is.

THE END

Want more of Nirandel, the world of dragons? Pick up the standalone fantasy, Of Dreams and Dragons today.
Also enjoy these books coming soon:
Vampire Girl: Christmas Cognac
River of Dreams (from the Nightfall Chronicles)
Ellabelle: A Moonstone Academy Prequel Novella (from our new Moonstone Academy series)

If you to connect with us more, join our KK Coven group on Facebook where we interact daily, do giveaways, and will be starting a book club. We hope to see you there!

$\mathcal{W}$ORDS

"AND WHEN VAR DIED, from his stomach spilled a thousand drag-
ons. They spread throughout the worlds, killing mankind and
feeding off their Spirits."
— The Valarata, Tablet eight

Chapter 1
TWO WORDS

EVERYONE HAS A WORD. That one word that encapsulates and
articulates so much of who you are, that on a Venn diagram
there would only be a sliver that falls outside the scope of
that word. Most people never learn their word, but it's out
there, waiting to be found. Waiting to be called forth.

I... I have two words. My first word, only because I

learned it first, is *hiraeth*. It's not even English—though the best words seldom are, so that should hardly be counted against it. I initially discovered *hiraeth* on social media, and it made me suck in my breath as something stirred deep within me. It's Welsh, and there's no direct translation into English, but it's defined as a kind of homesickness tinged with grief or sadness over a person or place that is lost to you. It carries with it a sense of longing, nostalgia and wistfulness, and it's an emotion that has weighed on me every day of my life that I can remember. Discovering there is a word for what I've always felt does help ease the sorrow some, but only in the way that identifying the monster helps ease the fear. It's still a monster. It still hunts you. But now you know its name.

My second word is so closely aligned with my first that it maybe doesn't count. *Saudade*—originating in Portuguese and Galician—takes *hiraeth* another step, though. It is often defined as "the love that remains" after someone or some-place is gone—or even if that person or place is still in your life, but it has changed so much that you mourn the past or future.

These words are my ghosts. They haunt me, teasing at my mind as I go about my day. And they are directly tied to a life I can't remember, because I never lived it. A life that could have been.

If my father hadn't died before I was born.

If my mother hadn't married Pat.

If fate had taken a swing at someone else the day I was born, instead of setting its sights on me.

And today, my ghosts are more active than usual as I count the change for my groceries.

I usually shop early in the morning usually, when the crowds at Safeway are shorter, but today couldn't be helped. We're out of too many things and the kids are hungry, so I came after running other errands, when the lines are long and people are tired and impatient and ready to get home to their families.

Women are trained from childhood to be polite, accommodating and docile. To make others happy before themselves. To be self-sacrificing and humble. Which is why, as the line behind me lengthens, and tired shoppers check their phones for the time and sigh dramatically, I feel guilt. Guilt that I have to count out the quarters and nickels and pennies I found in the couch to pay for groceries for the three hungry children at home. Guilt that I have to keep putting back items that push my total too high. Guilt that I couldn't do all the math and taxes and weights of produce in my head, thus saving everyone the hassle of waiting on me. Guilt that I have to use food stamps to cover what my couch change can't.

Guilt.

Because I'm making the people behind me wait too long.

The cashier, Martha, is a middle-aged woman who's worked here as long as I can remember. She's always been kind, and fast, and I try to pick her line whenever I can. She doesn't shame me with silent looks and frowns that others sometimes do, even without realizing it. She gives me a small, sympathetic smile as I help bag my groceries in reusable bags that have seen better days. One is so frayed I'm not sure it will survive this trip.

"You sure you don't need another bag?" Martha asks.

"Gotta make these work till payday," I say, loading up my cart.

She nods in understanding. "Hang in there, Sky. You know what they say… this too shall pass."

I give her the best smile I can muster and nod. "Thanks, Martha. Sorry about this."

She's already scanning the next customer's food though, so I leave quickly, hoping to get home before the kids.

Fall has settled into the bones of the little city of Ukiah, and today is colder than usual. Winter is indeed coming, though we feel less of a sting two hours north of San Francisco than most of the country. The wind whips around my face, freezing my nose and ears, as I push my cart through the expansive parking lot to my car.

I can smell the rain before it falls, but I have no way of covering myself or my groceries, and the deluge of water soaks me to the skin by the time I pop open the trunk. I make quick work of getting the groceries into the car, but the last bag doesn't survive the experience and rips apart in my hand, depositing my food onto the wet asphalt.

At least the rain is cover for the tears threatening to fall. I'm exhausted, overwhelmed and so very tempted to leave the food there and get home, but some of it's still salvageable. And this was our grocery budget for the week.

A few eggs are still in one piece, and the fruit is only slightly bruised. If I cut it up for a salad, the kids will eat it without complaint. Probably.

I grab whatever looks edible and deposit it on top of the remaining bags, then finally slide into my car, where I'm marginally more sheltered from the rain. When the engine starts on the first try, I offer a prayer of thanks to whoever's listening. The car's an old beater I got off Craigslist. It's missing a window, the heater doesn't work, and the engine looks like someone tried to repair it by blasting it with fire and hoping for the best. I taped now-soggy cardboard over the missing window, and that was the extent of my repair budget. Now I use the powers of manifestation and luck to keep the thing running.

One perk of living in a city that's only about five square miles, despite it being the largest city in Mendocino County, is everything is under ten minutes away.

I drive past the 101 onramp, past the Starbucks I can never afford but always look at with longing, and turn at the corner gas station. Our house is across the street from a park, near an elementary school. On the outside, it looks like every other house on the block. Remarkable only in how ordinary it is. The lower middle class dream, minus the white picket fence.

It's when I unlock the door and walk inside that the truth of my home life hits the hardest. That's where the shadows live, behind the closed doors and draped windows of houses that look like everyone else's. Skulk past the white-washed exterior and you'll find the rot fast enough. But most don't care to dig even that deep. They may smell the decay, but they don't want to deal with the reality.

The groceries are nearly put away when Caleb sprints down the stairs at full speed, nearly breaking his neck as he trips over the last step.

I don't know how I get from the kitchen to the living room so fast. Sometimes it's like I blink and am standing where I want to be.

I catch the six-year-old mayhem-maker before he kills himself, and nearly sob from relief when he looks up wide-eyed, and then grins like a little idiot. "That was amazing, Sky! Let's do it again."

I grip him harder before he escapes my arms, his black hair flopping over eyes almost as dark. "Oh no, kiddo. Not again. I need your help in the kitchen. Where's Pat?"

Caleb shrugs and runs back upstairs before I can stop him. I sigh and stand, my body feeling a lot older than its twenty-four years. I trudge upstairs and check Caleb's room. He's sitting on his disheveled bed playing with his toy fire truck and another toy car flipped over on its side. The fire truck races across pillows and blankets as Caleb shrieks in a high pitched squeal meant to mimic the sound of a siren.

"Look, Sky, it's you and Blake saving people," he says as the fire truck arrives to help the turned over car. He pulls out

136

two dolls dressed in nursing outfits and mimics them helping another doll that was thrown out of the truck. "This one's you," he says, holding up a female doll with brown hair.

I ruffle his head. "She looks just like me."

Caleb grins, putting his attention back on his truck as I look around the room.

Caleb shares the room with his teen brother, Kyle, and little sister Kara. I expected to see her in the crib under Kyle's bunk bed, but it's empty. "Caleb, where's Kara? And where's Pat?"

Caleb looks up from his truck. "Gone."

"What? Where? When?" I'm trying to stay calm, but my voice is rising in pitch and volume. How long was Caleb left alone? And why did Pat take Kara?

"I dunno. Just gone. They left when I got home from school."

I grip the doorframe so hard my fingers turn white, then take a calming breath. "Thanks, buddy." I ruffle his hair and leave him to his toys as I run downstairs.

The living room is a mess. Pat left empty beer cans on the coffee table, and cigarette butts on the ground. The litter box in the corner stinks to high heaven and the cat's food and water bowl are empty. "Marshmallow? You around, kitty?" I pull out a toy and dangle it, hoping the bell will entice the white fur ball from her hiding place, but nope. She's not interested in humans right now. I give up and clean out her litter box, refill her food and water, then grab a trash bag to clean up after the man who calls himself head of this family.

The kids are his.

I'm not part of this family.

Not really.

Pat makes that abundantly clear.

I rub at a bruise on my arm and stretch my sore back.

The dishes are done and the house is as clean as I can

make it by the time Pat returns with Kara. Kyle trails behind them and drops his backpack by the front door.

I don't bother telling him to put it away. Not today.

I storm over to Pat. "Where were you? How could you leave Caleb alone?" The anger has been boiling in me for hours, and I can't contain it anymore.

"Back off, you free-loader." Pat slurs the drunken words, but I don't need to hear him speak to know he's been hitting the bottle. Hard. His dark eyes are glazed over and there's a vagueness about his expression that is familiar. He sneers at me, his lip curling. "I knew you'd be home soon. He's old enough to look after himself."

"He's six, Pat! That's not old enough, that's child endangerment. And where did you take Kara?" When she hears her name she reaches for me, and I take the toddler from her father. She has snot all over her face, her cheeks are red from the cold, and she's not wearing a coat.

"She's helping me make a little cash. At least someone does." Spittle flies out of his mouth, hitting me in the face. "I swear, the only reason I still let you live here is because of the debt I owe your mother, God rest her soul. But the dead aren't much good to the living, are they?"

I hand Kara to Kyle and tell him to take her upstairs. Kara's face crinkles into a cry as she calls my name, her arms held out to me. Kyle frowns, wanting to stay and help, but I shoo him away with Caleb following behind. I don't want them around when Pat's like this.

"You let me live here because without me running this house and raising these kids, you'd lose everything, including the extra money you get from your social security for them."

I should have kept my mouth shut. I know better, especially when he's like this. Hard liquor rather than beer was his poison of choice today. I can smell it on him. And I know what that means.

But knowing changes nothing. I seem pathologically incapable of biting my tongue. A character flaw I would be happier without.

Sometimes, the anticipation of pain is worse than the pain itself.

When his fist flies at me, I feel the pain of its impact on my jaw before it lands. And then my whole face is on fire.

I fall to the ground, hitting my head on the sharp edge of the staircase as I fall. But I don't cry or scream. I've learned not to. The last time I did, Kyle heard and came to help, and ended up in the ER due to a 'terrible fall' that broke two bones. I won't let that happen again.

When I was a child, I always wondered why I never saw stars when I was hit. In cartoons they always saw stars, but I only ever saw darkness as my vision blurred and shrunk in on itself until there was nothing.

I always wished for the stars.

Pat stands over me, waiting. He knows I'll get up, despite conventional wisdom telling me I should stay put and wait for him to grow bored and walk away.

Another character flaw.

I get up.

And in that moment, something happens.

A light ignites in me, burning my skin from the inside out. Energy rushes through my body.

Pat takes an unstable step backwards. "What the—"

I take advantage of the moment and step forward. He dwarfs me in girth and height, but somehow I feel bigger, stronger, taller right now. "You will never hit me again," I say, my voice sounding foreign, distant, like someone else talking through me.

Pat stumbles back. "Get away, you freak. You creature. You're not of my blood. You're not of my kin." His face turns ashen, all color draining from him as he stares at me in horror. I know what he's seeing behind my eyes. I have seen it in his too often.

I point to the front door. "Get out. Now."

And to my utter shock, he listens. His drunk ass flees the house, the door slamming so hard behind him it rattles the walls. When it's clear he's not coming back anytime soon, I slump to the ground, hugging myself. I think of the power that just overcame me, and I tremble. Not because I don't know what happened.

But because I do.

Read NOW!

AFTERWORD

Thank you for committing to this journey with us. We have been writing in this world for a few years now, with seven core books, a very long fantasy standalone (Of Dreams and Dragons) and several novellas, and we love it. These last two books were created during a very challenging time for us. Lux's brother took his life while we were working on Unseen Lord, and Dmytry became very ill around the same time and was unable to work for a few months. After many tests we think we have gotten to the bottom of the illness—a serious gut bacteria we both ended up with—and we are on the mend with heavy doses of antibiotics and a lot of doctor visits.

Through it all, these stories kept us going. They might not be as long as the first five Vampire Girl books, but they are packed with just as much love, adventure and heart. This last book was especially poignant as we wanted to capture the sense of love, family and friendship that has sustained us during these hard time as we gear up for the holidays. Thus, we wrote a few extra epilogues to take you into the lives of other characters you've grown to love on this journey. We hope you enjoyed how this ended.

This isn't the end of Vampire Girl, but it is a pause. We have big plans for 2019, including working on more Nightfall stories, and bringing you a new world in Moonstone Academy. We hope you fall in love with these new characters and new stories. In the meantime, we are still committed to bringing Vampire Girl to tv or movies, and are working toward that end.

This series wouldn't be possible without you, our dear readers. And we love you for it. Thank you. And thanks for sticking with us through it all.

If you to connect with us more, join our KK Coven group on Facebook where we interact daily, do giveaways, and will be starting a book club. We hope to see you there!

Love, Lux & Dmytry Karpov Kinrade

PS, keep reading to learn about a new adventure that awaits!

Ellabelle

I live in the forest of the fairies and frolic with the nymphs. I talk with the owls and hear the rumors spread by ravens. But it is within the walls of the old stone castle that I hear that which is worth knowing. The lies and secrets, the human willy-nillys. Normally it is all just bubbles in the sunlight. Nothing more or less. Nothing bigger or smaller.

But things are changing.

I just need medicine for my owl. He is my home and my friend and the person who listens the most. He speaks in the voice of the ancients and knows my heart. But he is sick, and the robed ones in the castle have potions and liquids and vials of magic they steal from the earth and the sky and the water and fire, and so I will steal it back from them to make my friend better.

That is when I hear it.

That is when I know.

The still waters will be still no more.

***

Welcome to a world of magic. A world of mystery. A world of adventure. Welcome to Moonstone Academy, a new series from USA Today bestselling author Karpov Kinrade. Enjoy a peek into the mystical island of Moonstone, where nothing is at it seems, in this novella prequel.

ABOUT THE AUTHOR

Karpov Kinrade is the pen name for the husband and wife writing duo of USA TODAY bestselling, award-winning authors Lux Karpov-Kinrade and Dmytry Karpov-Kinrade.

Together, they write fantasy and science fiction novels and screenplays, make music and direct movies.

Look for more from Karpov Kinrade in *Vampire Girl, Of Dreams and Dragons, The Nightfall Chronicles* and *The Forbidden Trilogy*. If you're looking for their suspense and romance titles, you'll now find those under Alex Lux.

They live with their three mostly teens who share a

genius for all things creative, and six cats who think they rule the world (spoiler, they do.)

Find them online at KarpovKinrade.com

On Facebook /KarpovKinrade

On Twitter @KarpovKinrade

And subscribe to their newsletter for special deals and up-to-date notice of new launches.

~~~~~

If you enjoyed this book, consider supporting the author by leaving a review wherever you purchased this book. Thank you.

ALSO BY KARPOV KINRADE

In the Vampire Girl Universe

Vampire Girl

Vampire Girl 2: Midnight Star

Vampire Girl 3: Silver Flame

Vampire Girl 4: Moonlight Prince

Vampire Girl 5: First Hunter

Vampire Girl 6: Unseen Lord

Vampire Girl 7: Fallen Star

Vampire Girl: Copper Snare

Vampire Girl: Crimson Cocktail

Vampire Girl: Christmas Cognac

Of Dreams and Dragons

Get the OF DREAMS AND DRAGONS soundtrack: itunes
Amazon Spotify Google Play

Moonstone Academy (a new series coming 2019)

Ellabelle: A Moonstone Academy Prequel Novella

Get the SOUNDTRACK single for Moonstone Academy Amazon
Spotify iTunes Google

The Nightfall Chronicles

Court of Nightfall

Weeper of Blood

House of Ravens

Night of Nyx

Song of Kai

River of Dreams

THE FORBIDDEN TRILOGY (completesci fi thriller romance)
Forbidden Mind Forbidden Fire Forbidden Life **Check out our
lyric music videos and book trailers on YOUTUBE Here:** Karpov
Kinrade YouTube

Our ALEX LUX BOOKS!

Find all our Alex Lux books on Amazon HERE for those who enjoy
more steam in their story!

The Seduced Saga (paranormal romance with suspense)

Seduced by Innocence

Seduced by Pain

Seduced by Power

Seduced by Lies

Seduced by Darkness

The Call Me Cat Trilogy (romantic suspense)

Call Me Cat

Leave Me Love

Tell Me True

(Standalone romcon with crossover characters)

Hitched

Whipped

Kiss Me in Paris (A standalone romance)

Short Stories

Only Forever

Mirrors and Monsters

Secret

Sapphire Eyes

Our Children's Fantasy collection under Kimberly Kinrade

The Three Lost Kids series

Lexie World

Bella World

Maddie World

The Three Lost Kids and Cupid's Capture

The Three Lost Kids and the Death of the Sugar Fairy

The Three Lost Kids and the Christmas Curse

Made in the USA
Coppell, TX
31 May 2020

26754800R00085